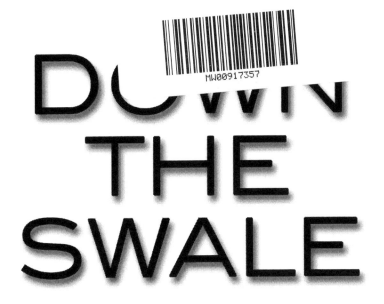

DOWN
THE
SWALE

VALERIE
MUNRO

Sagittarius Publishing
A Division of Sagittarius Media LLC
New Jersey

DOWN THE SWALE

Published by Sagittarius Publishing
A Division of Sagittarius Media, LLC
New Jersey

Library of Congress Cataloging-in-Publication Data (TK)

First Edition: July 2017

Produced in the United States of America

0 9 8 7 6 5 4 3 2 1

Acknowledgements

I would like to thank my sweet husband, Edward and my wonderful children, Nick and Tori for supporting me as a writer. You are the loves of my life and I am blessed to dwell with you beside the swale. Thank you for allowing me to spend time writing instead of doing the dishes and vacuuming.

A debt of gratitude is extended to author and editor Wil Mara, for not only his expertise and many hours spent on this book, but for true friendship and the sharing of many fine dining experiences including ribs in the smoker, crab legs, and cream puffs.

A heap of appreciation goes out to my students and your enthusiasm for reading. You inspire me to write and I am giddy with glee to have this book on the shelves in our school library!

Finally, to the 000 section of the library! Huzzah!

Dedication

For my Father...

And the dearest time we ever shared

At the closing of the Pequannock Branch Library

You instructed me to fill a cardboard box to the brim with books

Which were only five and ten cents apiece

On that day it felt as though you had bought me

A treasure chest

Full of gold and jewels

CHAPTER 1

In Trying to Do a Good Deed, Brogden Accidentally Goes Down the Swale

Brogden always knew he'd go down the swale (which, for those of you who don't know, is a shallow groove in the Earth that sometimes fills with water, old leaves, tiny dead things, and other nastiness). He just hadn't figured it would happen so soon. Rather, he'd planned that once he was old enough to make his own way, he'd pack up his belongings onto some sort of a rugged looking raft and bid a tearful goodbye to Aunt Gladys and Aunt Hazel—the tears being theirs, not his, of course. It would be the start of his life as a man. Years later, he'd return, head and heart filled with adventures, arms stuffed with gifts from the land below.

He never shared these thoughts with his aunts. They'd spent the greater part of his life lecturing him on the importance of staying clear of the swale. Aunt Gladys had told him no less than one hundred times that if his parents had stayed out of the swale, he'd have been raised by a mother and father instead of by two old ladies. "Not that we've ever minded, dear," Aunt Hazel'd always hastened to add.

Over and over again they'd rehashed that tragic day

when his parents, unaware of the danger of the approaching storm, had gone wading in the swale's shallow waters. His mother, Anuk, had held him under his arms while his legs dangled in the water. "You were kicking your feet and splashing away!" Aunt Hazel always laughed. And then, with very little warning, a fork of lightning had cut through the sky—at this point Aunt Gladys would wave her hands violently from side to side—and the heavens opened up! Then there was thunder! And sheets of rain slicing downward! And finally...incredibly...unimaginably—a flash flood in the swale!

Caught in the current, his parents' feet slid out from under them. They tried to make their way to the swale's bank, but the current was far too strong. Realizing their fate, his father had tossed his only son into the air. Brogden had hurtled toward the bank and landed into the lap of a very startled Aunt Hazel, who had been engrossed in capturing the image of a violet with her pinhole camera.

"Save him! Save him!" his parents had cried as the torrent swept them ever farther, until they could no longer be seen. Nor were they ever seen by anyone else again.
****

Because he had been so young at the time, Brogden had no memory of that tragic day. However, he often envisioned his parents coming back, climbing up and over the hill, rushing toward him. He tried to picture what his mother and father would look like if they were still alive. (And he preferred to think that they *were* still alive, just missing.) They'd be a foot tall. That much he knew, because that's how his people got their name. Foots. The foot-high folks.

Despite the circumstances surrounding his parents' disappearance, and despite the fact that, following their disappearance, his aunts immediately constructed a high brick wall on the banks of the swale to protect him, Brogden was fascinated by it. On days when Aunt Gladys was busy sweeping the floor of their hut under the wooden stairs, and on days when Aunt Hazel was preoccupied chasing black and orange spotted monarchs, Brogden would sneak down and sit up on top of the brick wall. He liked to watch things float by in the swale's brownish-greenish waterflow. Pebbles...small, perfectly round pieces of glass...sticks...leaves.... He had a hidden collection of colorful feathers, bottle caps, pennies and other curious items that he'd fished out, too.

The wide-awake smell of spring always lured Brogden to the swale. Throughout the winter, the flow was at a standstill, with everything frozen and hidden under piles of snow. But in spring the ice thawed and the things which had been trapped in that frozen-ness began moving along again.

One spring day, Brogden was seated on the top of the rock wall counting the small white-capped splashes as the water rushed merrily along. When the water was moving at such a brisk speed it was impossible to see anything in it. But it was pleasant to listen to, and the sun was warm on his face. Altogether it was a quite-nice experience, and it almost lulled him to sleep. In fact, just as his lids were about to close, a dot of red caught his eye.

It was a *gnome*! He had never seen one, but Aunt Hazel had described them to him during one of her lessons on Lake Wahkmo society. Foots like themselves were Hill-Dwellers. They could be found living throughout the hills above Lake Wahkmo. Many, like his family, lived in huts beneath wooden staircases or in rarely-used sheds. The House Dwellers were generally much taller (although their young did start out quite tiny) and they came and went in things called cars and trucks and used things called lawnmowers which could be deadly if a Foot wasn't careful. There were also the Roamers: deer, squirrels, chipmunks, skunks, opossums, and the like. And the Tree-Dwellers, which had wings and, according to Aunt Hazel, spoke in foreign languages, mostly in chirps and twitters.

But this was a creature of an altogether different variety. Brogden stared with fascination at the red-capped gnome, who was paddling down the swale in a tiny basket-canoe. He had a thin grey beard and wore a blue vest over his shirt, short trousers, white hose, and pointy brown boots. He methodically paddled first left and then right, with seemingly little difficulty. From time to time he stopped paddling to sip from a tiny acorn cup and pop what appeared to be small, oblong, brown nuts into his mouth.

It was while the gnome was tipping the cup back to take a drink that he failed to notice the two large speckled rocks which poked up side by side through the surface of the water, directly in his path. Brogden had often thought

4

about how much fun it would be to stand with one foot on each of those rocks and feel the water rushing beneath him! The space between the rocks would have allowed the gnome's basket-canoe to pass through had he entered the passageway head-on, but the canoe slipped in at a slight angle and the gnome quickly became quite thoroughly stuck.

"Well, isn't this just fine!" declared the gnome. He stood up and, without success, tried to shove off by pushing on the rock to his right. With considerable exertion, he tried the same thing with the rock to the left, but that proved no better. Defeated, he flopped down onto the bench inside the basket-canoe and began muttering to himself.

"Not good. Not good at all! Never going to make it on time. Going to lose my job. And on the first day!"

The poor gnome looked so distraught that Brogden felt sorry for him and called out, "Ahoy there!"

"What?! Who's there?" The startled gnome spun all around, searching for the source of the voice.

"Over here!" Brogden waved and scrambled down from the rock wall to the bank of the swale.

"Oh no! Not good! Not good!" The gnome's eyes darted from Brogden to a small, rectangular, brown box which sat on the bottom of the basket-canoe.

"No, it isn't good," Brogden nodded in agreement. "But I can help you get moving again. I'll be there in a jiff."

"No!" The gnome lifted his hand forcefully to halt Brogden who already had one foot in the swale. "Don't come any further!"

"It's no trouble at all," Brogden said, smiling. Both of his feet were in the swale. The water tickled his ankles as it flowed by.

"I can do it myself," the gnome insisted. "You see, I'm a delivery gnome. Up until today I've been on the tunnel dispatch, but an order came in from Lowland Lakeside, and Gordon was feeling poorly so I volunteered for the water route. Pays more, too. And with the little one on the way I can certainly use the money."

"Little one?" Brogden asked, unable to imagine what a newborn gnome looked like.

"Any day now," the gnome replied, throwing back his shoulders with pride. Then he seemed to recall the situation and snapped back. "I must get moving. Don't want to be fired," he said. He stood up and rocked the basket-canoe from side to side. His face turned a deep scarlet and beads of sweat began to run down his cheeks. But he continued undaunted. Brogden observed him with a mixture of curiosity and helplessness. Clearly the gnome was dead set against accepting any assistance.

"Ho! I'm spent!" the gnome finally called out after several minutes of trying. In the next breath he burst into tears. "I'm ruined! I *am* going to be fired! I'll be placed on the List of Banned and Disgraced Dispatchers!" He paused, thinking, and his face brightened for a moment. "Perhaps I can still get a job as a packager! But with the little one coming...oh dear...oh dear," he muttered.

"I am coming out to help you and that's final,"

Brogden declared. "Stand on!"

The gnome sat instead, picked up the wooden box, placed it on his lap and wrapped his arms firmly around it. "Okay then," he said, "But just a shove off is all. You may not, under any circumstances, touch this box."

"What would I want with your box?" Brogden called out. He was now almost upon the basket-canoe.

"What is it that you think we delivery gnomes deliver?" He stared in disbelief at Brogden. "Geez, I thought everyone knew!" He put his finger to his lips and looked nervously from side to side to be sure that no one was listening. "It's treasure," he whispered.

"Really?" Brogden replied. He was at the basket-canoe now, and he gave a great shove backwards on its bow. It didn't give at all.

"Oh dear! You can't do it either!" the gnome wailed. "I am ruined!"

"Now just hold still," Brogden instructed. "I'm going to push as hard as I can to back you out. Once you're clear, steer hard to the left so your canoe doesn't slip back in."

As Brogden was giving the directions, a cloud moved in front of the sun, and the sky darkened to a slate-gray.

The gnome, still gripping the box, squinted as he looked upward. "We'd better hurry," he warned. "Looks like a shower is on the way."

Brogden shot a wary eye at the sky. "Let's hope not," he said. "A swale can be a dangerous place in a storm.

Get ready to steer."

Once again Brogden put his hands on the front of the basket-canoe and dug his heels into the bottom of the swale. The water flowed down against his shins as he pushed forward.

"Push!" yelled the gnome.

Brogden pushed. He pushed until he felt the muscles in his arms and legs stretching and burning like fire. However, when at last the bucket-canoe finally began to wiggle slightly, his feet began to lose their grip on the bottom of the swale.

"Push harder!" hollered the gnome again, and Brogden began to realize that the gnome was more than a little bossy.

A clap of thunder drowned out the gnome's shouts. It rumbled around and around Lake Wahkmo before echoing away. The resounding eeriness sent shivers down Brogden's spine.

"Hurry! Hurry!" the gnome pleaded. A jagged streak of lightning was quickly followed by another clap of thunder, closer and louder. Then, from far off, Aunt Gladys began calling.

"Brogden! Brogden!"

She always called for him when a storm started up. Both she and Aunt Hazel liked knowing where he was. Most of all, they liked knowing that he was *not* in the swale...which was why he didn't answer her.

"You are going to have to help me!" Brogden told the gnome. "Stand up and shove off the rocks while I push from behind!"

"No," the gnome refused. He sat firmly. "*I am not letting go of this chest!*"

"Well then, you'll be stuck, because I'm not going to stick around here any longer. This swale is about to become a mighty, roaring river! I don't think I can get you out and then get myself out of the swale in time. We'll both drown! You must help!" Brogden cried desperately.

"*Brogden!*" Aunt Gladys' voice was growing nearer and more frantic. "*Brogden!!!*"

A fork of lightning, white and electric and sizzling, flickered directly above them. Then a boom of thunder caused them both to jump. A gigantic raindrop hit Brogden square in the middle of his forehead, almost knocking him backwards. All around them, huge splashy drops pattered the surface of the swale. *Plap! Plish! Plash!* Two more drops caught him, one on his right arm, and one which drenched his mop of long hair so completely that he had to sweep it out of his eyes. Even then, it was difficult to see with the raindrops falling so forcefully. The water in the swale was beginning to swoosh by quicker and had already risen to his knees. From somewhere above, but not too far away, Brogden could hear a rushing sound and he knew that he only had minutes to spare.

"Stand up!" he ordered at the top of his lungs. Something in his tone must have been particularly forceful, for the gnome finally, although still very reluctantly, set his treasure box on the floor of the basket-canoe and got to his feet.

"Now push off!" Brogden commanded. "On my count!"

The water had risen past the tops of his knees and was splashing into his face. All sorts of leaves and rough-ended twigs were caught in the current, too. They scratched his legs and arms as they were swept downstream. Brogden was afraid to open his mouth to speak again for fear of it filling up with rain and leaves and bits of branches and God only knew what else.

The gnome put his hands on the rock to the left. Brogden tightened his grip on the slippery bow of the basket-canoe.

"One!"

A flash of lightning.

"Two!"

Aunt Gladys and Aunt Hazel reached the bank of the swale, their faces paled with fear as they caught sight of him in the swirling water.

"*Three!*"

Later, he would try tried to figure out which it was that did the trick—the added strength of the gnome, or the giant wall of water that hit like a tidal wave, that freed the basket-canoe from between the rocks. Perhaps it was the combination of the two, he mused.

In the end it didn't matter. The basket-canoe broke loose and flew downward at startling speed. Brogden tried to grab hold of it in order to rescue the gnome, but he (the gnome) had been knocked off his feet, and the last Brogden saw of him were his tiny hands clutching the treasure box as he was swept away.

Brogden turned to try to make his way back to the bank, but then a wave slapped him full in the face. Knocked off his feet, his body jostled and bounced along out of control. He tried to raise his head for air, but each time he did so, another wave shoved him under and further down the swale. He continued tumbling along, rain-soaked head over aching heels over flailing arms over scrambled legs. There was no way he could have seen the huge, jagged rock in his path until he was just upon it. His body crashed into it with a fury equal to that of the storm itself. His final thought before everything went black was that his aunts' worst nightmare had become a reality.

He had gone down the swale.

CHAPTER 2

AFTER EXITING THE DRAINPIPE, BROGDEN BECOMES CAPTAIN OF HIS OWN VESSEL

When Brogden came to, he was shocked—not to mention very relieved—to find that he was still alive. His body was sprawled at an odd angle, and from where he lay he couldn't see where his right foot was. He wiggled where he *thought* the big toe of his right foot might be and cried out in pain. From the knee down, the leg was twisted under his backside.

"At least it's there...." he moaned.

For a moment he couldn't recall what had happened, then it all came rushing back—the storm, the gnome, the stuck basket-canoe, his aunts' panic-stricken faces, and, worst of all, the river of water that had carried him down the swale presumably to the spot where he lay now. There was no sign of the gnome, either. Still afraid to move for fear of shooting pains firing off in other parts of his body, he remained still and glanced about at his surroundings. He was lying in about an inch of water in a round, silver drainpipe. The water flowed slowly from a source overhead, continued past him, and dropped off about three or four feet ahead. He could hear its splashing, like a quiet waterfall. The drainpipe's exit was a bright yellowish circle of light, and it was quite blinding after he had been unconscious for so long. Droplets of water hung down from the top rim of the pipe. Sunlight hit the droplets and sent rainbows dancing all around. Then the droplets fell and were quickly replaced by more droplets, and the colorful display continued. It was all quite beautiful to look at, and Brogden would have lain there all day had he not been in so much pain.

"Help!" he called out.

The plea echoed through the pipe—*Help...elp...elp....*

"Please! Someone help me!" he tried again. *Help me...elp me...me....*

He wasn't surprised that no one answered his cry. After all, who else would be hanging around in a drainpipe? And with that thought, Brogden knew he would have to rescue himself. Gingerly he turned his body so as to free his leg, and stabbing pains shot through his ankle, causing him to grimace in agony. He pushed upward on his palms, and, sitting upright, began to inspect the damage to his foot, which he also noticed was now shoeless. The outside of his ankle sported a large, throbbing rosy-colored ball that was rapidly changing to a plum purple color right before his eyes. There was no question in his mind that his ankle was sprained at the very least.

A terrifying realization interrupted his inspection of the injured ankle. It was a miracle that he hadn't been pitched from the drainpipe into the lake! The thought of *that* sent shivers up and down his spine, and he decided that, despite the condition of his ankle, it was not safe for him to remain here. He must get out of the drainpipe before another deluge came along.

He stood up, wincing as he put weight on his foot. Gripping the side of the drainpipe with one hand to balance himself, he removed the other shoe. It was a spring shoe that Aunt Gladys had patterned after a pair of House Dweller's snowshoes and was constructed from tightly thatched oak and maple leaf stems. Although the one shoe would most likely be useless and somewhat bothersome to tote around, he didn't want to leave it behind. Tying the laces together in a loop, he pulled it up his arm and over his shoulder, then limped through the shallow water toward the opening of the pipe. His clothes—knee-length breeches and a tunic—clung heavily to him. Every few seconds he stopped to lean against the side of the drainpipe and wipe the mop of long hair from his eyes.

As he limped to the drainpipe's entrance, the light became brighter and the dripping louder. The rows of dripping droplets made it difficult for Brogden to see outside. When he finally reached the end of the pipe, he held onto the sides and stuck his head out. Water dripped onto his neck and down his back, but as he was already soaked through, he paid it no mind.

He had indeed reached Lake Wahkmo, and the drainpipe he was in ran several feet over it. The lake water was constantly moving, and its colors morphed from a dark piney green to grayish blue. And above it all, a shimmering layer of gold sunlight danced and sparkled. Brogden also noticed that some House Dweller children were noisily chasing ducks on the small, sandy beach alongside the drainpipe.

A faded wooden dock stuck out from the beach, and he could see a few boats tied up nearby. Brogden knew a little bit about boats. Aunt Hazel had once taken him on a hike to Balanced Rock and pointed out the motorboats that House Dwellers used. The House Dwellers could be seen traveling up and down the lake from late spring to early fall. "Bow riders, because they can ride in the bow, or front, of the boat," she'd explained. Brogden guessed that there probably wasn't anything better in the world than to ride in the bow of a boat with the wind on your face.

It was hard for him to decide what his next course of action should be. While he knew that he certainly couldn't remain in the drainpipe, he wasn't sure where else to go. It was a short drop into the water, but he had never swum before. He also had to decide which direction to go once he was in the water—toward the beach or out to the dock. The beach was farther than the dock, and he'd run the risk of being seen by the children. (And after witnessing their relentless pursuit of the ducks, he wasn't eager to have that happen!) The dock was closer, but the flashing, silver propellers on the boats looked menacing. He didn't want to get too close to them, either! The best thing would be to find something to float on, he thought, and then he could move away quietly. Unfortunately, the water below him was filled only with brown feathers, which he figured must have come from the ducks. His head turned from side to side as he tried to make up his mind. *Beach.... Dock.... No.... Beach.... Wait.... Absolutely not.... Dock....*

Just as he was about to jump, hope for the best, and make up his mind once he was in the water, a blue plastic Frisbee flew through the air. It zipped right in front of the drainpipe and almost cut off his nose. It landed in the water directly below him and floated on the surface There was writing on it, but since Brogden didn't know how to read, he had no idea what it said. Besides, the top of it was touching the water and facing away from him so he would have had to read not only upside down, but backwards as well (which would have been difficult for anyone). Had he been able to read, he would have seen that it said "For the Best Ice Cream Cones in the World...Come to the Milk Barn" with a phone number underneath.

"*Grandmaaaaaaaa!*" A little girl's voice rang out. "Rory lost the Frisbee! He threw it over there!!!"

Peeking out, Brogden saw a skinny, freckly girl wearing overalls that were rolled up to her knees. Her auburn hair hung down in two frizzy braids, and she was pointing her little finger in the direction of the Frisbee. A gray-haired woman rose from the lawn chair where she had been reading a paperback book. She was in blue jeans and a frayed camel-colored sweater, and there was a sun visor propped on her head. She joined the girl at the edge of the sand where it met the water.

"See!" the girl whined, still pointing. "It's the second one he's lost this week!"

Rory, the culprit—who was a near-perfect copy of the girl, minus the braids—joined them.

"S'not my fault she can't catch," he grumbled.

17

"S'not true!" the girl spat back. "You can't *throw!*"

The three stood looking at the Frisbee.

"I can get it, Grandma!" Rory said. "I'll just climb up on that drainpipe and reach down."

Upon hearing that, Brogden moved farther back into the drainpipe, afraid that he would be discovered. He could, however, still hear what they were saying.

"You can't reach it from there," his sister argued. "You're too short and you'll fall in. 'Sides, Grandma says the water's too deep over there. See? It's outside the ropes!"

"But I can swim!" Rory cried emphatically. "I'm a good swimmer!" He was clearly excited at the prospect of attempting this dangerous recovery mission.

"No, that Frisbee will have to just stay put," Grandma stated firmly. She pointed at the sign on the beach. "See? No swimming on the beaches for another week until the lifeguards are on duty. Those are the rules of Lake Wahkmo."

"Aw, rules shmooles," Rory pouted.

"I'm sorry, but that's the way it has to be," his Grandma said. "Now, we'd better head back to the house. I've got a nice pot roast waiting for us, and you two can help me set the table before Grandpa gets home." Her voice trailed off as they wandered up the beach.

When Brogden felt sure they were gone, he poked his head out. The Frisbee was still floating there. He surveyed the beach. There were just two children left, but they were busy on a swingset, pulling their legs back and forth as they flew through the air.

Brogden had now come to the conclusion that the Frisbee was his best option for rescuing himself. With his head tilted to one side, he pondered how to best get onto it. He eventually figured that his best course of action would be to sit on the bottom of the drainpipe and shove off with his hands. That way, he'd most likely land on his bum, not on his still-aching ankle.

So that's what he did—and quickly discovered that someone sitting in the upright position when they jumped would not necessarily remain upright when they landed. He hit the Frisbee on his side, and had to scramble to right himself before the Frisbee, which he realized was terribly tipsy, turned over. Once he was upright again, he also discovered that this did not guarantee staying afloat, either. So he tried various positions. If he sat too close to the edge of the Frisbee, it began to tilt up behind him, and he had to move back toward the middle to steady it. He tried sitting on his knees, and lying down on his stomach with his legs hanging off one side. He also tried lying flat on his back with his legs hanging off the other side, but that seemed awfully unproductive (although he did spot some interesting cloud formations from that position). He finally sat with his bum square in the center and his legs sticking out in front of him. That proved to be most satisfyingly stable.

And it was while he was seated this way that a marvelous thought occurred to him—for the first time in his life, he was captain of his own vessel, even if it was only a plastic blue Frisbee. Although he knew that his first order of business ought to be coming up with a plan to get home to his aunts—who were probably out of their minds with worry—he couldn't help feeling a sense of…well, a sense of adventure!

"The world is mine!" he proclaimed triumphantly, and a fantasy of sailing across Lake Wahkmo settled in his mind until he realized that, although he had something of a vessel, he did *not* have a sail, an engine, or a propeller. (Suddenly the propellers on the boats didn't look *so* menacing. Actually, they looked quite *useful*.) Then he recalled his shoe, slung over his shoulder. Perhaps it could be used as a kind of oar?

He wound the laces around and around the shoe and tied them together so that no part of them hung down. Then he began paddling to his right. After several strokes, he found that his hard work only resulted in the Frisbee spinning around in a circle, which made him a bit dizzy.

He waited until spinning stopped, and tried a new tactic. He paddled one stroke to the right, then one to the left. Right…left…right…left…as quickly as he could. After several minutes he was red in the face, out of breath, even more dizzy, and virtually in the same spot where he'd started!

Discouraged, he pulled the shoe-oar out of the water. He realized now that without a current to push him forward, he'd be going nowhere. And at the moment, there wasn't any current to be found.

He looked again at the propellers on the boats. *That's what I need—some kind of propeller!* Maybe his feet would work...it wouldn't be that hard. If he stayed in his seated position and kicked, he'd move in reverse (which was not altogether a bad thing, and at least he'd be moving somewhere). *But what about the pain in your ankle?* his brain reminded him, and he was forced to admit that a set of foot-propellers was very much out of the question. Holding his shoe on his lap, he sat and sighed over his terrible state of affairs.

If only he could make it to the dock, he thought, he could hide in one of the boats for a day or so while his ankle healed. Then he'd head to the beach, hike to where the drainpipe met the swale, and follow the swale home.

The boat dock was probably only twenty feet away, but to Brogden, who was all of a foot tall, it felt like twenty miles. He would have remained there bobbing up and down like a cork for who knows how long had not two ducks skimmed into the water beside him. They created an impressive splash, drenching him all over again and almost causing his Frisbee to overturn. (He was beginning to wonder if he would ever be dry again!)

"Quack quack quaddle," said the larger of the two ducks, who was the male. Brogden knew this because of the green head.

"Quaddle quaddle quack quaddle," replied the smaller female, who was covered only in brown feathers.

Brogden hadn't the foggiest idea of what they were saying, and he was feeling more than a little uneasy at being so close to ducks. The only birds he'd ever known were a family of disruptive woodpeckers who hammered away at the willow tree near his home, two bossy blue jays, and a tiny robin. He'd enjoyed the company of the robin best of all. He'd found the beautiful sky-blue egg in a tiny nest hidden deep in the bushes and had befriended her as soon as she'd hatched. Each day he'd brought her small, pink wriggling worms to eat. They'd had delightful talks and grew quite fond of each other, so it came as a terrible disappointment when the robin's mother indicated that that an ongoing friendship would not be possible once her youngster began to fly. He had sadly reported the news to Aunt Gladys.

"Birds are too unreliable," she'd said. "Never in one place for long. That whole migrating business," she'd frowned. "And I can't understand a thing they say."

If Brogden had understood the quacking of the ducks that were paddling near him now, this is what he would have heard:

"I'm sick and tired of being chased by those kids all day!"

"Me too! And I am *starving*. Do you think we'll find a fish?"

With that, the second duck flipped upside down. Her brown and white speckled tail, feathers, and webbed feet waved in the air. Brogden watched in utter fascination as the duck remained that way for almost a minute. When she flipped upright again, a tiny silver fish dangled briefly from her beak before it disappeared.

"Quaaaack?" The first duck asked which meant "A minnow?"

"Quaddly quaddle quaaaaaaak!" the other replied, which meant "Yes, and tasty too!"

Following this conversation, the first duck did likewise, flipping upside down. However, he lacked the finesse of his female companion. His webbed feet teetered from side to side as he dabbled. Brogden watched as the duck's feet moved closer and closer to the Frisbee until the duck was three feet away...two feet away...just inches away.... Brogden was about to risk further injury to his ankle and kick himself out of reach of the duck, but it was too late. He yelped out in pain as the duck's beak clamped down on his toes!

CHAPTER 3

BROGDEN STOWS AWAY
ON THE *ALMOST HOME*

"Hey!" Brogden hollered, and yanked both of his feet up onto the Frisbee. "Watch it!"

The duck righted himself abruptly and looked about, his head turning from side to side.

"Who? What? Where's the fishies?" the duck squawked, in English this time.

Brogden stared in wonder. Up close he could see that the duck's head wasn't solid green after all. It was beautifully iridescent and mixed through with gold and violet. Bold violet feathers adorned his sides.

"You..." Brogden sputtered as he pointed at him. "I..." he choked out. "I can understand what you're saying!"

The duck spun around and faced him.

"Whoa!" the duck screeched. He burst into a string of quacking and began swimming nervously back and forth. "Quaaaaaaaaack! Quackle quackly quackly quackster!" Several times during his tirade he pointed at Brogden with his wing. Brogden remained seated on the Frisbee, shielding his toes with his hands in the event the duck decided to take another bite.

"Quacker! Quackee! Quacko!" The duck's noises

became more feverish, and it was clear he was growing more disturbed by the minute. The female began swimming alongside and stroking him with her wing.

"What's the matter?" Brogden called to her. "What is he saying? Can you translate?"

"He's in a dreadful state," she replied (also in English, and also to Brogden's utter astonishment). "He's saying that what appeared to be five fat fishies weren't fishies at all. He says that they were the terrible tasting toes of an odd little man!"

Brogden didn't know which to be more offended by—the notion that his feet were offensive, or that a duck had called him odd. After a moment's consideration, he decided he was more disturbed by the latter.

"Odd?" he retorted with a huff. "What you mean odd? It would have been considerate of you to watch where you were going, and whose toes you're nibbling on!"

The duck (whose name Brogden presumed was Fred due to the fact that the female kept saying "Calm down, Fred," and "Go to your happy place, Fred," and "Breathe, Fred, breathe.") kept up the pacing—or, rather, swimming—back and forth, muttering, "Deeply distressing. Deeply distressing." Brogden watched this for several minutes before deciding that Fred was acting like a baby and completely overreacting.

"Oh puh-*leez*, what is so distressing?" Brogden asked.

"Quackly, quackly, quackly," Fred answered.

"He says he's never seen a gnome before," the

female translated. ".He says he'd always believed gnomes were imaginary. He says he thinks he's losing his mind."

"Why now, that's just plain silly," Brogden declared. "I'm not a gnome at all. They are much, much tinier. I'm a Foot," he stated proudly, pulling himself as tall as he could while remaining seated. "Foots are a full foot tall when fully grown. And," he added, "You never need to fear a Foot. We are kind and gentle."

Fred stopped swimming and turned toward Brogden.

"You don't chase ducks? You don't throw rocks or sticks or try to poke ducks with cattails?" he asked.

Brogden shook his head. "Most certainly not!"

Upon hearing this, Fred appeared to calm down considerably, and extended a wing to Brogden, who shook it gently.

"So sorry," Fred said. "You see, my wife Nancy and I are not from this area. We have flown in from Lake Wannalacka. Both born and raised there. We married this past fall. A splendid ceremony with all sorts of waterfowl attending. Ducks. Geese. Even *SWANS*," he emphasized with great importance. "We planned to live out our lives there on that peaceful lake." The top of his green head turned a shade darker as he became more incensed. "And then, this spring, just as Nancy was getting ready to lay her eggs, something dreadful happened. People came to the land near our cove and cut down all the trees so they could build houses. Soon there was nowhere left for us to build a nest, let alone live with the grinding sounds of bulldozers and saws and power drills."

"It was quite disturbing, as you may well guess," Nancy chimed in.

Brogden had never heard of a 'bulldozer' or any of those other things, but it did sound unpleasant, so he nodded his head empathetically. He also unshielded his toes, convinced that they were not in any further danger.

"We had no choice but to depart from our beloved home," Fred continued. "We flew for miles, searching, asking around. A wise old owl suggested we try Lake Wahkmo."

"It's very beautiful here," Nancy said. "But we have been plagued by children chasing us at this beach and haven't had a moment's peace to build a nest. Perhaps we got it wrong. Maybe the owl meant another lake," She shook her head. "Poor Fred. His nerves are just on edge. And I guess meeting someone so…well…unusual looking…just threw him for a loop."

"Yes, but I feel so much better now that I know you are not out to harm us," Fred said. "You haven't told us, Mr. Foot, why you are out here on your round floating vessel?"

"You can call me Brogden, as that is my name, and how I came to be here is quite a tale,"

Both ducks turned around and looked quizzically at their tails.

"No, no," Brogden laughed. "A tale. A story. Let me tell it to you."

He lay down on his stomach across the Frisbee,

leaned his front half up on his elbows, and told them every bit of what had happened, starting with the gnome and ending with the trouble involved in steering a Frisbee. The ducks listened attentively, except for Fred's occasional dabbling. ("It's not that he's not interested, dear." Nancy explained apologetically. "It's just that he's a constant snacker.")

Brogden finished by telling them about his plan to make his way to the boats and find one in which to stow away for a few days before heading home.

"Sounds like a good plan," Nancy agreed. "Your aunts must be worried sick."

Brogden smiled and glanced at the sky. The sun was beginning its descent now, and as much as he was enjoying the conversation with the ducks, he didn't want to spend the night on the Frisbee. He needed to get to the boat dock before darkness fell. Nancy followed his gaze and patted Fred's shoulder (or at least where a shoulder would be if ducks had shoulders.)

"It's getting late, Fred," she said, "and we must let Brogden be on his way. And despite the number of rambunctious kids that keep chasing us at this beach, I would like to check out that clump of bushes." She indicated a spot near the beach with her wing. "I'd like to see if it's a suitable nesting spot. I do believe I will be laying eggs in the very foreseeable future."

Fred smiled proudly.

"Brogden, my foot-friend," Fred said. "It would give me great pleasure to provide you with transportation to the boat dock," he offered. "Free of charge, of course."

"Why, thanks! I'd really appreciate that!" Brogden exclaimed. Sitting on the Frisbee was exhausting. The whole time he had been talking, he still had to concentrate on keeping the Frisbee balanced—and that was every bit as stressful as it sounded.

"A few nudges in that direction would be fine," Brogden said.

"Certainly not!" Fred cried. Then, to Brogden's great surprise, he bowed his head, which turned his neck into a kind of ramp. "Climb aboard and I'll give you a float!"

If only Aunt Hazel could see me now, Brogden thought as he carefully climbed on top of Fred's back. He was going to leave his shoe behind on the Frisbee, then thought the better of it and stuck it under his arm. He gave the Frisbee one backward glance as they left it behind.

Riding topside on a duck was a strange and wonderful sensation. Fred's outer feathers had a thin, slippery coating of oil, and it gave Brogden the feeling that he might slip right off and into the water.

"Squeeze your knees against my sides," Fred instructed. "You can wrap your arms around my neck too."

"Really? Won't that hurt?"

"Not a bit," Fred said. "Go ahead."

With his arms encircling Fred's neck, Brogden thoroughly enjoyed the ride. Fred's webbed feet moved like paddles beneath him, and he made tiny quacking sounds as they glided through the water. Nancy trailed alongside, quacking her own soft tune. They traveled much quicker than Brogden would have thought possible. He turned around and saw a perfect V-shaped wake fanning out behind them. Then, all too soon, the delightful ride ended—they had arrived at the boat dock.

The boats looked much larger to Brogden than they had when he was still on the Frisbee. Words were painted on the back ends, and Fred explained that each boat had a name. He swam by them slowly, and Nancy read the names out loud. Brogden was very impressed with how learned the ducks were.

"*Lazy Daze...Reel Time...Seas the Day...Our Toy....*" Nancy read. "*Yachts of Fun...Summer Breeze...Sea Phantom....*" Do any of these seem appealing to you?" she asked him.

"Not really," Brogden admitted, and he saw that there were two more boats in slips on the other side of the dock. "Can I trouble you to float by the ones over there?"

"No trouble at all," Fred said. Then, without warning, he flipped upside down to dabble again, and sent Brogden flying off into the dark water!

Brogden kicked wildly as he begin sinking fast. From under the water he could see Fred snap up a silvery fish. He found it hard to keep kicking and kicking. Straining to push upward by pushing downward with his shoe, he almost reached the surface, then drifted back down. He kicked hard again. He needed air—*air...I need air...*—and then (*hallelujah!*) he felt himself being picked up by the seat of his pants.

Nancy lowered him gently onto the wooden dock,

and Brogden gulped air into his lungs.

"Poor thing!" Nancy cried. Then she turned to Fred. "Whatever were you thinking?!"

"I'm so sorry," Fred apologized. "But I couldn't help myself. Instinct, I suppose. Terribly sorry."

"It's okay," Brogden told him, but inwardly he was glad to be back on the dock! The two boats were just a few feet from where he was sitting. "Well, I guess it'll be one or the other," he said. "What are these called?" he asked Nancy.

She swam over behind the first boat—a small blue bow rider with a gray cover.

"This one is called the *White Knuckle Express*," she said. She then proceeded to paddle over to the other— another bow rider, which was white with blue and gold pinstripes. "This one says *Almost Home*."

Well, Brogden could have just about burst into tears—of joy, mind you—right then and there. He knew that he wasn't almost home, and that it might very well take him days to find his way back. But this boat gave him great hope!

But he was also overcome with tiredness. And with the sun almost fully behind the hills, all he wanted to do was find a dry place to lie down.

"I guess it will be *Almost Home*," he said aloud. Then he hesitated, unsure of how to leave the ducks. "Err—I don't suppose you'd like to stay here as well?" he asked.

"Goodness no!" Nancy said. "We need to be

outdoors, in the open, swimming freely."

"With the fish!" Fred reminded him.

"But thanks just the same," Nancy added.

Brogden nodded. "Well, thank you for everything," he said.

"You're welcome," Fred said. Then he added sheepishly, "And I'm truly hoping you'll forget about the business…you know, with your toes."

"No harm done," Brogden told him. "Well, goodbye then!"

He watched as the two ducks paddled slowly away in the direction of the beach. Then he turned back to *Almost Home*. He walked gingerly down the plank next to the boat, putting as little pressure as possible on his ankle, for it was still in great pain.

He saw that there was a cover snapped onto *Almost Home* in several places all around. He also realized with some anxiety that he couldn't reach *Almost Home* from the dock. There was perhaps two or maybe even three feet of space between the dock and the boat—much too far for someone his size to jump. He had no desire to be in the water again, especially without Nancy there to rescue him. However after further inspection, he saw that thick ropes held the boat securely in the slip, two in the front and two on the sides. They were tied to metal rings on the dock's wooden planks. Another rope was also tied to a hook in the front of the boat and secured at the front of the slip.

He decided that his best chance at safely boarding *Almost Home* would be to climb across one of the side ropes, because they were the shortest. When the boat stopped moving about in the restless water, he took a deep breath and, holding his shoe in his teeth, grabbed hold of the rope with one hand. He stepped off the plank and hastily reached for the rope with his other hand. The rope dipped slightly, and he swung freely between the plank and the boat. Then he made his way to the boat by reaching one hand over the other. When his side bumped against it, he held on with one hand while feeling overhead for the snap on the cover with the other. After a few tries he located the snap, but it was secured much tighter than he had anticipated. He pulled mightily, but it wouldn't come free, and he was quickly losing the strength to hang on with just one hand.

The dark water churned menacingly beneath him, and for a moment he almost gave up hope and dropped into it. Then, with a sudden burst of energy and desperation, he planted his feet on the side of the boat's hull, reached up with one hand, and grabbed hold of the silver cleat that the rope was wrapped around. Finally, he pulled himself up awkwardly over the top of the boat—and then collapsed onto the cover! He spat out the shoe and lay there catching his breath.

From this position, he discovered a few moments later, it was much easier to undo the snap on the cover. With his first pull, it came free with a most satisfying sound.

"Now we're getting somewhere!" he cried triumphantly. He climbed under the cover and onto the top of a seat. Then he reached up and tried to snap the cover shut again. But it was a nearly impossible thing to do from the inside, and he gave up trying. Seeing how dark it was now, he realized he'd be grateful for the sliver of light that snuck in anyway.

His ankle was feeling a little better, but his stomach was most decidedly not—a rumble reminded him that he hadn't had anything to eat or drink all day. His first order of business, therefore, would be to scavenge around for some food. He slid down the seat and onto the floor of the boat, feeling his way around. An exploration of the boat's right pocket revealed a red fire extinguisher, a black-handled flashlight, several orange life preservers, and a few coils of white rope. The left pocket held more life preservers, a long wooden pole with an orange flag at one end, and a half-filled water bottle. Brogden promptly opened the bottle and gulped down the contents.

He felt somewhat better after the drink but was still ravenously hungry, so the search continued. In the glove compartment he found an owner's manual, a whistle, a bottle of sunscreen, a pair of white sunglasses with huge round lenses, a pack of gum, and a first aid kit. Inside the first aid kit, to his relief, was a long bandage and a pair of tiny scissors.

He used the scissors to cut off a small piece of the bandage. Then he wound it around his ankle and secured it with a piece of white medical tape. Now the ankle felt so much better.

Next, he tore open a piece of the gum and popped

it into his mouth. He'd never had gum before and wasn't sure if he should swallow it or just chew it. Based on the feel of it, he opted for just chewing. It had a nice cinnamony flavor, but it did little to quiet his rumbling tummy. However, he was pleased with the small comforts that he had already found.

He thought about the name of the boat—*Almost Home*—and smiled. He could wait until tomorrow to deal with his hunger, he thought. But all in all, he was in a much better situation than when the day began.

Bonk! Bonk! Bonk! Bonk! Bonk!

A series of loud taps against the boat's hull suddenly grabbed his attention.

Bonk! Bonk! Bonk! Bonk! Bonk!

Brogden's heart caught in his throat as he wondered who could possibly be doing this. No one except Fred and Nancy knew that he was hiding in here!

Cautiously, Brogden climbed back up to the top of the seat and slowly lifted the cover. Peering out into the darkness, he saw that the moon had begun to rise.

Bonk! Bonk! Bonk! Bonk! Bonk!

There was the tapping sound again—but he could see no one.

"Down here, Brogden!"

He looked down to find Fred and Nancy floating in the water between the plank and the boat. Nancy had been tapping with her beak.

"Whew! You sure gave me a scare!" he told her.

Fred held up a plastic baggie in his beak. It was

filled with bright orange cheese doodles.

"We found these on the beach," explained Nancy. "And we thought you might be hungry."

"I wanted to bring you a fish," Fred said.

"Oh no, these are just fine," Brogden replied. He didn't say so, but he was very glad it wasn't a fish.

"Very well then," said Fred. "If you just reach out, I'll fly them on up."

Brogden leaned out over the side of the boat as far as he dared. Fred gave a great flap of his wings and rose up into the air next to the boat. After Brogden retrieved the plastic bag from Fred's beak, the duck dropped splashily down beside Nancy.

"Thank you!" he called down to them.

"Sweet dreams!" Nancy sang out, and then they flew off.

As Brogden pulled the baggie of cheese doodles inside the cover, he stole one last look at the moon. He could also see the stars of the Big Dipper. He and Aunt Hazel always searched for the Big Dipper at home, and he wondered if she was doing that tonight. Just knowing that she might be looking at the same stars as him gave him some comfort.

He shimmied down the seat and set the baggie on the floor. He wanted to poke around the bow of the boat before he went to sleep. It was almost pitch black in here, so he ran his fingers along the seat cushions and discovered that they came to a point in the front of the boat. He also discovered that, with considerable effort, he was able to lift the seat cushions upward. There was a hidden compartment beneath it.

He found more rope, two oars, and a woolen blanket. He brought out the blanket and constructed a cozy bed from one of the orange life preservers. After getting under the blanket, he re-opened the baggie of cheese doodles. They felt a little soggy and smelled a little fishy (having been carried in Fred's beak and all) but were, on the whole, very satisfying.

Covered with orange crumbs, with the remaining shoe tucked under his arm, and with thoughts of home drifting dreamily through his mind, he lay there listening to the beautiful-yet-mysterious sounds of Lake Wahkmo until he drifted off to sleep.

CHAPTER 4

BROGDEN AND HIS NEW NOCTURNAL FRIEND HEAR A WARNING

Brogden had been asleep for four hours (which felt like much less) when he was awakened by a scratching sound and a string of high-pitched squeaks. His eyes popped open and he sat upright, listening carefully to the sounds. They started and stopped every few seconds, and seemed to come from a different place above him each time. It seemed to him like something, or someone, was trying to get underneath the boat's cover. In fact, he could see that whatever or whoever was making the noise was making little dents as it ran around the cover. Brogden found this downright creepy as he watched from underneath.

He recalled that when he had said goodnight to Fred and Nancy, he had not snapped the cover shut. That had been for two reasons. One, he was petrified that he would run out of air under the cover. And two, he didn't want to be in total darkness. Back at home, in his hut near the swale, he could always look out and see the House Dweller's garden lights, which came on at dusk every evening. And of course, he had his aunts to keep him company.

Brogden knew that it was only a matter of time

before whatever or whoever it was discovered the opening by the snap, and he prayed the creature wasn't dangerous. Then he thought it would be a good idea to find something he could use as a weapon. *Just in case....*

He climbed out of his bed and found the flashlight. He figured that if the creature managed to get underneath the cover, he would startle it by shining the light directly in its eyes. That might even be enough to make it run away. The flashlight could also be used to pack a heavy punch. (Brogden had never punched anyone in his life, so he was hoping that things wouldn't come to that.) He stood there alert, flashlight at the ready, watching the shifting cover, as whatever or whoever it was came closer and closer to the opening. He could hear it trying, without success, to lift the snaps on the cover.

"Darn! Darn!" a voice grumbled. The cover shifted again and Brogden knew it was attempting to undo the snap next to the open one.

"Darn! Darn! Out of luck! This one's stuck!" The voice was louder and closer now. Finally, as Brogden had predicted, the cover shifted as whatever or whoever it was reached the opening.

"Snap snip snap! Snippety rap! JACKPOT!"

The cover flew up and moonlight streamed in, temporarily distracting Brogden, and he forgot about his plan to turn the flashlight on the intruder. When his eyes adjusted, he looked up and found himself staring into a small, pointy white face with two dark, beady eyes!

"Grrr! Grrr!"

The creature emitted a low growling sound, clearly unhappy to be taken by surprise.

"Grrr! Grieee! Grieee!"

The snarls became higher pitched as the eyes bore into him.

"Gree-Yeeeee! Yeeeee!"

With ear-splitting shrieks, the creature began wriggling its way into the boat. Brogden raised the flashlight and shined it directly into its face, revealing pointy teeth! Lots of them! Directly above him!

"Be gone!" Brogden shouted. "Away!"

The noises stopped and the creature made no further move. The black eyes continued their accusing stare as its tiny pink nose twitched back and forth.

"Off! Off with you!" Brogden demanded again and took a step forward. The flashlight teetered as he held it high in what he hoped looked like a menacing pose.

"A-kitch! A-kitch!" the creature said. Then, without warning, it began sneezing violently. This startled Brogden so much so that he began to back away, trying to put some distance between them. It was a good thing he did so, because after the fourth or fifth sneeze, the creature appeared to lose its footing and fell straight down into the boat. It lay motionless on its side at Brogden's feet!

When he was able to see the body that was attached to the small white face, Brogden felt quite silly and relieved. It was an opossum, and appeared to be a very young one at that. He'd learned all about opossums from Aunt Gladys.

"The ridiculous blokes," she'd said. " Overly dramatic, if you ask me. They lie there like they are as dead as a doornail, causing everyone to go into mourning like they really are dead. Why, I've heard of entire funerals being held and beautiful eulogies given on account of such shenanigans and then, just before the burial..." she'd paused, shaking her head in disgust, "the opossum...comes...alive...again...causing everyone to go into a state of shock and hysteria, as you can well imagine! *And*," she'd sneered, "those prehensile tails! Ugghh!" Brogden had listened to all of this with great interest, but felt her comment about the tails was really not fair. It wasn't as if creatures could control if they were born with a prehensile tail or not. He actually thought prehensile tails were quite interesting.

But, thinking again about an opossum's ridiculous habit of playing dead, Brogden gave the animal absolutely no attention. Instead, he turned away and began humming a tune that Aunt Hazel had been singing lately called "Oh, the Spring in Splendid Glory!" He was well into the last line of verse three ("And the honeysuckle swe-et!") when he glanced sideways and caught the opossum opening one eye and stealing looks at him when he thought Brogden wasn't looking! It was just as Aunt Gladys had said. The opossum was...well, playing possum.

So Brogden began a new tune, this one with a peppier beat than the first. It was called "The Syncopated March of the Millipedes", which Aunt Gladys had deemed absurd, stating that you couldn't possibly march to a syncopated beat. But Brogden liked it and found that he could march to it if he kept a steady beat by snapping his fingers. It was a snazzy tune.

"I like that one better!" the opossum suddenly called out and rolled into a seated position. "It's nice and jumpy. Do keep going!"

Upon being complimented, Brogden launched throatily into the remainder of the verses, and the opossum's prehensile tail swayed back and forth as he kept time. He ended by crooning a series of arpeggios and gave an encore performance of the chorus (and a half-step higher at that).

"Bravo! Bravo!" The opossum clapped his paws together enthusiastically and stood for an ovation.

Brogden bowed deeply and sat down cross-legged next to the opossum. The furry creature extended a front paw for a shake.

"Fourteen," he said.

"I only have ten," Brogden smiled and held up both of his hands, displaying his fingers.

"No, no," the opossum explained. "That's my name. Fourteen."

"That's a number," Brogden said.

"True," the opossum agreed. "I'm one of fifteen brothers and sisters, which is not at all unusual for opossums. We are marsupials you know. When we're born, we aren't any larger than bees, and we do much of our growing in our mama's pouch. Well, after about two and a half months it gets awfully squishy in there, what with everyone's elbows and knees bumping into everyone else's backs and tummies. Well, there simply wasn't any more room for us in the pouch, so Mama invited all of the relatives over for "Exiting Day". It's the traditional big day for opossums when we all climb out of the pouch and onto our mama's back. Our whole extended family showed up for the event. Up until that point, nobody had even seen us or knew exactly how many of us there were."

He paused for a second to remember more of the details, twitching his little nose from side to side.

"When my first sibling exited Mama's pouch," he went on, "everyone cheered. It was a boy, and naturally, he was named after my father. My second sibling was a girl and when she exited everyone clapped," he went on.

"She was named after your mother?" Brogden guessed.

"Of course," Fourteen said. "Our exiting continued with whistling and hooting and stomping and the throwing of confetti as we were each named after a relative. Then we lined up on Mama's back," he said.

"Who were you named after?" Brogden asked.

"Great Great Uncle Oliver," he replied. "Being as I was squished near the bottom of the pouch, I exited second to last. All the really good names like Rocky and Vinny were taken," he sighed wistfully. "As it turned out, it really didn't matter. That was the first and last time my mother ever called me Great Great Uncle Oliver. With fifteen of us to take care of it was impossible for her to remember who was who," he said.

Brogden nodded. "I can imagine."

"'Sam', she'd say pointing to Joe, and Sam would say 'No Mama, that's Joe, I'm over here.' She mixed up Frankie with Herman and Carly with Shelly and never could remember Janey who had been named after a very distant cousin. It became worse and worse. Downright confusing. Things became so bad that at one point that we were all forgetting our *own* names having been called by the wrong ones so many times. We were spending most of our days arguing over who was who, and finally Papa suggested that we just keep the family names for the first girl and boy, and give everyone else a number. So Papa hung us up by our tails on a branch and gave us a number. And that's how I became Fourteen."

"Wow," said Brogden, who was an only child and couldn't imagine having so many brothers and sisters.

"Fifteen wasn't called Fifteen though. She was called Baby." Fourteen hung his head. "Sometimes I do wish that I had a real name."

"What name would you choose?" Brogden asked.

Fourteen sat thinking and twiddling his thumbs.

"I didn't like my *first* real name—Great Great Uncle Oliver—but I wouldn't mind being called Ollie," he said, brightening.

"Ollie it is then," Brogden declared. "And I'm Brogden. By the way, you haven't said why you are here."

Ollie went on to say that although his family was on the whole, a jolly and loving bunch, the burrow that they all lived in was very cramped. There was hardly anywhere to sleep, and he was always one of the last to get any food.

"So I've decided to strike it out on my own," he said. "This beach has been ideal because the House Dwellers who come here are quite messy. They leave all kinds of snacks behind when they head home for the day. Chips, pretzels, crackers, and if I'm really lucky…*chocolate.*" He said this dreamily and patted his stomach. Brogden thought he saw a line of drool drip from the corner of Ollie's mouth.

"Yessirree," Ollie went on, "it's been a paradise. And now that it's spring, some of the boaters leave scraps behind, too. That's why I was trying to get into the boat," he confessed. "I'm so sorry if I scared you. Why are *you* here?" he asked.

Brogden told Ollie everything, from his unplanned tumble down the swale, to the drainpipe (he held up his bandaged ankle dramatically), to the Frisbee, to his encounter with Fred and Nancy, to stowing away on the boat.

"I'll be heading home first thing tomorrow," he ended.

"That's good to hear," said Ollie. "Because…well…I don't usually buy into local gossip, but I've been hearing some strange whisperings about this lake."

"What do you mean?" asked Brogden.

"Well, for one thing, *this*…." He scooted over the top of the seat to the opening of the boat cover and stuck his head out. His large ears swiveled around. Then he motioned to Brogden and said, "Come here, quick!"

Brogden climbed up next to him, poked his head out of the opening, and listened. The night sounds of the lake were a cacophony of bird calls, cricket chirps, and cicada songs.

"What is it?" Brogden asked. He couldn't pick out anything specific.

"Listen harder," Ollie said.

Brogden did the best he could, and beneath all of the other sounds he could hear croaking, which seemed to be coming from the tall reeds on the far side of the beach. The croaks had been there all the time, but with all of the other sounds, they'd just blended in. The longer he listened, the more the croaking began to drown out the other sounds. He realized that the croaks were words!

"Danger! Danger!" The croaks were saying. "Danger! Danger!"

A wave of fear washed over Brogden, beginning with the hairs on the back of his neck and traveling all the way down to his toes. His hands felt slick and clammy, and a queasy sort of feeling took hold of his stomach. *I'd give anything to be home with my aunts in our hut under the wooden staircase next to the swale right now*, he thought. He moved closer to Ollie, who, sensing Brogden's apprehension, wrapped his tail protectively around his shoulders. It gave Brogden a small sense of comfort.

"What does it mean, Ollie?" whispered Brogden. "What is the danger? Fred and Nancy didn't tell me about any danger."

"But you did say that Fred and Nancy were new to the area," Ollie whispered back. "So they probably didn't know. All the locals have been talking about there being some kind of danger for weeks now."

"Ollie…" said Brogden. "Can you…I mean…will you stay here in the boat with me? Just till the morning?"

The opossum twitched his little whiskers back and forth as he considered the request. The frogs were still croaking their warning.

"Well, I don't see why not. It's just one night…but…uh… the truth of the matter is that I'm nocturnal. That means I'm awake most of the night, and I sleep during the day. Are you nocturnal, too?"

"No," Brogden admitted. "Actually I was asleep when you got here."

"Well, seeing as how being nocturnal is part of who I am, I won't be able to go to sleep," explained Ollie.

"Well, maybe, perhaps you could…" Brogden began, trying to think of a solution. Anything to convince Ollie to stay. He didn't want to be alone with an unknown danger lurking about.

"Count sheep?" Ollie guessed. "Been there. Done that. Last time I tried that, I was well into the thousands as the sun was coming up."

"Oh," said Brogden. "Well, that's okay. I can fall asleep quick as a wink. I won't even hear you if you're scurrying about. I'd just feel better knowing that someone is here, what with those frogs going on about danger."

"Okay, I'll stay—if you're sure that I won't be a

bother," Ollie agreed. "I certainly wouldn't want anything to happen to you."

Ollie pulled the cover taut, until no light came in at all. Laying back down on his lifejacket bed with the blanket up over his head, Brogden was unable to hear the croaks. He held onto his shoe until he drifted off.

To his credit, Ollie did try to sleep. He lay on the floor near the seat where Brogden was sleeping and for a while, all was still. But after a short time feeling restless, an urge to get up and move about overcame him, and he began to scurry around the *Almost Home*. He paced up and down from the bow to the stern, and ran laps on the bow seats. He wrapped his tail around the steering wheel, hung upside down, and swung back and forth. He fiddled with the radio dial. He explored every nook and cranny with his twitching nose and whiskers. But in the end it was hunger pangs that made him leave. He could wait no longer to rummage near the trash bins on the beach, and just before dawn, he popped open the cover and scuttled out of the boat.

CHAPTER 5

A Real Boat Ride for Brogden Proves Very Dangerous Indeed

A ray of sunlight fell across Brogden's face and mop of long hair. It was bright enough to rouse him from what had been a deep but disturbing sleep. In his dreams, he had been alone on Lake Wahkmo, spinning around and around on the blue Frisbee, in the center of a circle of lily pads. A huge frog sat on each pad and called out "Danger!" He spun faster and faster, and he was about to go flying off the Frisbee when he woke up.

"Whew!" he sighed, thankful that it had just been a dream. He blinked and shielded his eyes with the back of his hand.

The opossum was gone, he noticed, and his stomach was talking again. It was saying that it felt like days since he'd eaten the soggy cheese doodles, and would he kindly do something about getting breakfast? If he were home with his aunts, he'd be settling down to a nut cake with some thick, gooey blackberry preserves spread on top. Aunt Gladys would be going on about the nutritional value of the blackberry, and Aunt Hazel would be asking if he preferred spending the day hunting for the seven-spotted lady bug (a particularly lucky insect) or painting a watercolor of the fairy ring in the meadow. The fairy ring was a large circle of mushrooms that the meadow fairies rested their feet upon following their dancing celebrations.

"Well, the porch needs to be swept and there is dusting to be done before anyone goes hunting or painting," Aunt Gladys would most likely say.

The breakfast would be topped off with a steaming mug of willow-bark tea—and remembering this, Brogden's mouth now began to water. Then he realized his aunts were probably not even eating breakfast, as they would most likely not have slept a wink. Aunt Hazel's eyes would be red-rimmed from sobbing, and Aunt Gladys, with her pragmatic sense of order, was probably making a list of the exact steps they should take to locate Brogden. And thinking about that is what spurred him to get up and moving.

Luckily, the swelling on his ankle had gone down. When he lifted the edge of the bandage with his thumb and forefinger, he could see that the injury had taken on a yellowish-purple hue, with a hint of green around the edges. The sight of it made him queasy, so he covered it again. When he stood up, he realized quite happily that it looked worse than it felt. A dull ache remained, but it wasn't sore enough to prevent him from getting on his way.

Aunt Gladys' daily regiment of chores had instilled in him the value of organization, and he quickly set to work returning all of the things that he'd used to where he'd found them—the life vest, the blanket, etc. He had to push on the cushions quite firmly to get them back into place. Then he went about straightening up until things were just as they'd been when he'd gotten there, except for the empty baggie from the cheese doodles. He figured that he would fold it up and take it with him, as it might make a good sort of a raincoat.

Just as he reached for it, he froze.

Voices! House Dweller *voices!*

He could hear them faintly through the boat's cover, but had no idea how far away they were. It sounded like the shouting of young children, as well as an older, deeper voice.

Brogden thought back to the night before, when he had been approaching the dock on Fred's back and tried to remember exactly how many boats there were. The odds that the voices he was hearing now just happened to belong to the House Dwellers who owned *Almost Home* were low. Perhaps one out of eleven or twelve, which wasn't terrible odds. Besides, he reasoned optimistically, luck was usually on his side (except for the nasty fall down the swale and ending up far away from home in a boat in a lake where there was possible *danger!*). But despite those dreadful circumstances, hadn't things worked out so far? He *had* managed to escape the drainpipe and find shelter and make a few new friends. Years ago, when some rogue squirrels had broken into and then stolen a great deal of their winter's store of nuts, Aunt Hazel had pointed out that at least their cupboard was still half full. He'd learned from her to look on the bright side of things.

The voices were coming closer now. And although they still somewhat muffled by the cover, Brogden could distinguish a boy's voice.

"Dad, why's she gotta bring a *doll* on the boat? Dintcha tell her *no dolls* on the boat? She's getting too old for dolls. She's almost ten!"

Then a girl's voice—"I can *too* bring this doll. You get to bring *your* stuff!"

"Yeah…well…what if your dolly fell in the water?"

Brogden heard a scuffling and what sounded like several thuds.

"Give it!" the girl shrieked. "I say, give it back! Daaaaaaaaaaaaad!"

Brogden could tell that the House Dwellers were getting closer, and he prayed that the boat they were speaking of was *Lazy Daze* or *Yachts of Fun*. *Any boat but this one*, he thought.

"Knock it off, Emory," said the man, sounding slightly annoyed. "And I could use some help uncovering the boat."

He couldn't explain how or why, but in that moment Brogden knew that the House Dwellers weren't headed to any other boat. They were going to uncover *Almost Home*—and then they were going to find him!

He looked around desperately, his heart pounding like a drum, but there was nowhere to hide. The best idea he could come up with was the compartments under the seat cushions—and with surprising swiftness he snatched his shoe and raced to the front of the boat. Using both hands, he tugged with all of his might and was able to raise one of the cushions just high enough to squeeze into the space below. He landed with a soft *whummp* on the blanket that he had used during the night and then reached up and yanked the cushion down over his head.

The inside of the compartment was dark and musty and filled with a brackish odor that was not entirely pleasing. The thick air made it difficult to breathe, and his ragged panting echoed off the sides of the compartment. He was sweating already and prayed that he wouldn't have to be in these confined quarters too long.

Just as he was wondering exactly how long he would have to stay there, the boat gave a sudden lurch. He was thrown onto his side, and it took all of his courage to keep from crying out in fear. The boat rocked from side to side, and he could hear the water splashing against the bow. He gripped the corner of the blanket and listened to the muffled voices and the vibrations of feet pattering all around the boat.

The seat cushions were insulating everything so he could only catch bits and pieces of the conversation. He thought he heard things like "Ewwww! What's this!? Did a mouse get in here?" and "Run the bilge," and "Turn the fan on," after which he did hear an airy sound coming from somewhere very near him (which made it harder to hear than before). After what seemed like hours, he heard and felt a mighty rumble. He knew it was just the engine, but it was still terrifying. And it didn't help that he was experiencing it in the dark under the seat cushion.

Then a somewhat pleasant realization crossed his mind. He *was* going for a boat ride for the first time in his life! The cupboard was half full! More than half full! *Wait until I tell Aunt Hazel*, he thought excitedly. Boating was simply luxurious, Aunt Hazel had said with a dreamy far-off look in her eyes as they'd watched the boats together while sitting on Balanced Rock.

Brogden heard the man barking orders.

"Unhook the back! Pull up the fenders once we're out of the slip! Atta boy! We're off!" The boat jerked into motion, and Brogden reached for the side of the bow to steady himself as it reversed out of the slip and turned. He then felt *Almost Home* move slowly forward and heard the man's voice say something about a 'No-Wake Zone.'

It was a wonderful sensation, Brogden mused, to be gliding along the water, listening to it lapping rhythmically against the sides of the boat. He was right in the middle of envisioning exactly how he would describe the experience to Aunt Hazel when he was suddenly thrown backwards! The boat leaped into the air at a steep angle as it took off, accelerating at lightning speed. He clung to the blanket for dear life. Then *Almost Home* leveled off again and Brogden found himself righted once more.

Back and forth, up and down Lake Wahkmo it went, only slowing the breakneck pace when it reached its destination. Then *Almost Home* leaned on its side as it circled around. Each time it entered the arc, Brogden was thrown on his side. And as much as he tried to stay in a seated position, the force kept him pinned until, with a jolt, it would take off again. After the first few runs, and after his initial fears were dispelled, he grew used to the speed and the turns. It was thrilling!

"Faster!" he heard the children cry with delight. "Faster!"

Almost Home shifted into a different gear and shot forward even quicker. How Brogden longed to be *on* the seat cushions rather than under them, feeling the wind in his hair and the spray in his face!

He counted a total of six times up and down the lake before the boat came to a stop. He felt the wake push it forward as it settled into place. Then it sat bobbing gently. Even in the dark, he could tell that they weren't back in the slip at the dock. His guess was that they were somewhere out in the middle of the lake. He decided to take a chance and push the seat cushion up the tiniest bit so that he could get some fresh air and see who the bold captain of the boat was. The cushion made a teeny squeaking sound as he lifted it, and he prayed that it didn't attract anyone's attention.

He breathed deeply as fresh air wafted through the opening. The sunlight that had awoken him was gone—now he saw only gray clouds in the sky.

He spied the captain at the steering wheel, a tall man with gray curly hair and tan, weathered skin. He wore a faded blue baseball cap and round wire glasses. The man was staring at something in the distance and seemed oblivious to the brown-haired, freckle-faced boy and girl who were calling to him repeatedly. Clad in bright orange life vests, they were bouncing up and down on their seats in the stern.

"Dad! Dad!" they called. "Are we going to ride in the tube now? We really want to go in the tube!"

How different the boat looked in the daytime! Brogden thought. The seats were bright white with bold blue striping. Tan carpeting covered the floor, and the windows were so shiny-clean that they gleamed. Behind the children, tied onto a platform in the stern, sat a large, round, red-and-yellow inner tube. The children kept casting hopeful looks at it.

Finally their father turned to them.

"By the look of this sky, you may as well get some tubing in now," he said. "I heard a new batch of storms will be moving in later today."

"I'll tie the tube on, Dad" the boy offered eagerly.

His father held up a hand to still him.

"Wait just a second, Emory," he said. He pointed at the gas gauge. "We certainly don't want to get stuck in the middle of Lake Wahkmo waiting for a tow. You and Amy can tube after we gas up. We'd best head over to the marina."

From the hiding spot, Brogden watched Dad push down on a black lever, and the boat began moving forward. Then Dad spun the steering wheel and swung the boat around. That caused Brogden to lose his balance and fall backwards onto the blanket. He'd been feeling just a little seasick, and the sudden lurch didn't help. The boat traveled for about a minute, then slowed to a crawl and stopped.

Brogden peeked out again. The motor was still running, and they were sitting in a line of boats in front of a white building. Brogden assumed this was the marina that Dad had mentioned. The paint on the building was peeling so badly that there was more exposed wood than anything else. Swallows darted in and out of the building's overhang, bringing food to chicks that were waiting in their mud nests up in the rafters.

There were at least forty boat slips at the marina. Most of them stuck out from a dock into the lake, but several were under the marina's overhang. A number of people were in their boats, tinkering and talking. Two gas pumps sat on the dock, and a few boats were lined up nearby, waiting for their turn to get their tanks filled.

Dad steered *Almost Home* into the last place on the line.

"There's Finnegan!" yelled Emory, pointing to a small, curly haired dog who was seated in the bow of the boat in front of them.

"Hi there, Finnegan!" Amy called. The dog turned and barked a hello. Then he turned back and stared straight ahead. Every so often, Finnegan would lift his black nose and sniff the air. His owner, an older man with white hair and a stubby beard, waved a greeting, and Dad and the kids waved back.

When it was their turn to pull up to the pumps, Dad cut the motor, and a tall man who looked as old as the marina itself reached out from the dock with a rope. He tied a knot around one of *Almost Home*'s back cleats, pulled the rope taut, and tied the other end to a metal ring on the dock. When the boat was secured, Brogden saw the man walk across the back deck of *Almost Home* with the fuel hose. He unscrewed the lid of the gas tank and guided the nozzle into the hole. The numbers on the fuel pump began to roll, making a dinging sound at the same time.

"How's it going, Varick?" Dad asked the man.

"To be awake is to be alive," Varick replied, and he did so in a way that gave Brogden the impression he used this saying all the time. "That's Thoreau," he told the kids with a wink. "One of the greatest authors ever."

Varick's weather-beaten face and twinkling eyes looked as though they had remained unchanged for many years. No one knew how long he had been employed at the marina, nor where he came from. Folks said that he'd been a sailor who'd served most of his life in the Navy. Certainly that explained the many tattoos on the muscled arms that stretched out from his sleeveless shirt: dragons, palm trees, an anchor, a dagger through a rose, and a red ribbon with the name Maria written across its slithering form. It was said that Varick showed up at the marina years before on a rainy day with just a sack on his back and was hired on the spot as the marina manager. Every day, for as long as anyone could remember, he showed up early in the morning and didn't leave until after dark, when he would walk into town and catch a bus. When he wasn't working on one of the boats brought to the marina for repairs, he would sit on the dock by the gas pumps in a plastic chair, reading a book.

"Hey Varick, is it true that there's a monster in Lake Wahkmo?" Amy asked. "The kids at school say it is."

The numbers on the pump came to a stop. Varick removed the nozzle and screwed the cap back onto the tank. Dad handed him two twenties from his wallet, and Varick disappeared inside the marina office to get change.

"That's just ridiculous," Dad scolded her. "Don't bother Varick with such a silly question."

"But..." Amy interrupted.

"But nothing. You are getting too old to be worrying about 'monsters-under-the-bed' stories," said Dad.

"Not under the bed," she corrected. "In the lake! Like a sea serpent!"

Brogden was watching and listening to all of this with great interest when Varick returned with two dollars, which he handed to Dad, and two chocolate bars, which he presented to Emory and Amy.

"Save these for after lunch," he smiled. They thanked him and promised to do just that.

"Well?" pressed Amy.

"Well what?" said Varick.

"What about the monster?" Amy repeated.

"Wellll... you know," Varick drawled. "These hills and this lake are full of magical and unusual creatures." When he winked, Brogden froze—it seemed like Varick was looking straight in his direction!

"Be serious, Varick!" Amy pleaded.

"Listen closely," said Varick. He untied the ropes that had secured *Almost Home* to the dock and gave them a shove off. Dad started up the motor again, and Brogden had to strain to hear Varick's words above the noise. "Everything you can imagine is real!" he called out as they began drifting away.

"Thoreau?" Dad guessed.

"Pablo Picasso," Varick smiled.

Dad attached a long pole with an orange flag to the boat, and they spent the next half hour crisscrossing the lake. Emory and Amy took turns riding in the tube. Brogden felt slightly seasick especially during Dad's wide turns, and decided to lie down on the blanket and close his eyes. Soon enough, he reassured himself, Dad would bring *Almost Home* back to the dock, and then he'd be able to climb out and head home.

Finally, *Almost Home* did come to a halt. Brogden slung his shoe over his shoulder and readied himself to climb of out of the compartment. But his heart sank when he hoisted himself up and peered out from under the cushion. They weren't back at the dock—*Almost Home* was sitting in the center of the lake! Dad cut the motor, turned the fan on again, and opened the hold where the anchor was stored. Brogden ducked down and hid as Dad strode to the front of the boat with the anchor in hand. He slowly lowered the mushroom-shaped weight by the long length of rope that was attached to it. When the anchor hit bottom, the rope stopped unraveling and Dad knotted it around one of the front cleats. Then he walked back and switched on the radio.

"You kids enjoy the water," he announced. "I'm going to read the paper." He sat down, stretched out his legs and turned to the section marked 'Business.'

"Last one in is a rotten egg!" Emory shouted, and cannon-balled off the stern. Amy followed close behind. They began splashing each other, flapping their arms like wild chickens, shrieking and squealing with delight. Brogden thought it looked like great fun.

The sun climbed high into in the sky. Dad finished reading the Business section and went next to World News. Emory and Amy grew tired of cannonballs and began a new game where each one tried to look like a letter of the alphabet as they jumped into the water.

Emory held his hand in a fist above his head and yelled, "Lowercase i!" before plunking off the swim deck.

"Capital Y!" Amy followed with her arms outspread above her head.

They completed the alphabet three times and started on numerals. Dad finished reading both the World News and the Local News by this time. He was just starting on the editorials when Brogden noticed that his eyes were drooping. Perhaps it was the warmth of the sun. Perhaps it was the gentle swaying back and forth. Nevertheless, by the time the kids were on 15 (a tricky double jump requiring both of them) Dad's eyelids were most decidedly closed.

It was at this point that Brogden was overcome by the urge to escape the confines of the dark compartment. The compartment was just so stuffy, and he'd developed a crick in his neck from craning it upward. And since Dad's eyes were shut, he concluded, it just might be safe enough to sneak out for a few seconds. He'd never been in the middle of Lake Wahkmo before (and probably would never be again), so he wanted to check out the view.

Brogden counted slowly to fifty and continued watching Dad's eyelids. They remained closed. Next, he shot a look over at the kids. They were totally engrossed with belly flops. Shouldering his shoe, he made his move.

As quietly as possible, Brogden pushed up on the cushions to widen the opening. It made the same squeaky sound as before, and he hesitated. But Dad did not stir. Brogden gave a final shove and scrambled out into the open. He headed to the forward-most point of the bow and turned his head all around. The view was breathtaking in every direction! The hills surrounding Lake Wahkmo rose up gently on all sides in brilliant, lush greens. Looking northwest, he could see the full length of the lake. It made him feel very tiny indeed.

He stood there a long time, taking it all in, committing to memory the way the waves began on one side of the lake and traveled like long wrinkles to the other side with nothing to stop them except their own energy, which curled over them in whitecaps. His eyes swept across the sky and marveled its vast openness. It made him want to throw his arms open wide and inhale deeply. Never in his life had he seen anything so enormous. Back home, the view of the sky had always been obscured by trees.

As he was standing there contemplating exactly which adjectives he would use to describe the sight to Aunt Hazel, a prickly feeling ran up his arms. He had the uneasy feeling that somebody was watching him. Slowly, he turned around to find Dad staring directly at him! His jaw hung upon and his face was pale as a full moon.

"M-m-monster!" he croaked, pointing a shaky index finger at Brogden. "A little monster!"

Brogden stood in place, utterly terrified. His first impulse was to try to run back to his hiding spot beneath the seat cushions. But his feet seemed stuck, as though they were attached to deep roots.

"It can't be...I must be seeing things," Dad muttered to himself. His newspaper had dropped from his chest to the floor. He removed his glasses and rubbed his eyes with the back of his hand. Then he polished the glasses with a corner of his shirt and put them back on. Brogden hadn't moved a muscle.

"It's still there!" Dad yelled.

Emory and Amy had just climbed up the ladder onto the swim deck.

"What's still there?" Emory asked while he dried his hair with a towel.

"The little monster!" Dad hollered.

"Little monster?" Amy echoed, not really understanding.

"There! Right there!" Dad was ranting like a madman and pointing at Brogden, whose heart was fluttering faster than a pair of hummingbird's wings.

"Ooooh! It's a little man! A cute little man!" Amy cried out and immediately lunged forward with outstretched arms in an attempt to grab Brogden.

"No! He's mine!" argued Emory. He pushed past

her, nearly knocking her down. The two children became entangled and fell to the floor, causing the boat to rock unsteadily back and forth.

Dad reached out to stop them. "Don't touch it!" he warned them. Then, to Brodgen—"Get out! Go away!"

Brogden didn't need to be told twice. Emory had gotten back on his feet and was now holding a long-handled net, which was kept in the boat for fishing.

"Don't move," Emory whispered. "Just...stay...right...there...."

Amy crept behind her brother, elbowing him in the ribs as she tried to get around him.

"He's *mine*, I tell you! *I* get to keep him when you catch him. *You* have a turtle. I don't have any pets!" she demanded.

Brogden's eyes darted left and then right as he frantically looked for a place to go. Back inside the compartment was no good, for that meant certain capture.

The net loomed closer.

"Hold still now...." Emory murmured, his eyes glittering.

"Get him! Get him!" Amy pleaded.

"I'm going crazy!" Dad cried. "Lack of sleep, lack of vitamins, too much stress...." he rambled.

"Al...most...there...." said Emory. The net hovered above Brogden's head, only about a foot away now. Emory whooped and brought the net down with a mighty thud, yelling, "I've got him!" But in fact he didn't—Brogden had sidestepped to the left, and the net crashed to the floor.

"Dang!" yelled Emory, although his parents strictly forbade cursing. (It was close enough to *not* cursing, he figured, even if they didn't see it the same way.)

He raised the net and brought it down again, but Brogden had jumped to the right this time.

"Get him! Get him!" Amy squawked.

"Get *away*!" Dad wailed.

The net crashed down again and again, and Brogden skittered around like a mouse to avoid capture.

"Stop!" he pleaded. "Stop it!"

"Ooooooh! He *talks*! I want a little man that talks!" Amy whined. "Do hurry up and get him!"

"I'm trying!" Emory snapped back. "But he won't stand still!"

Brogden clambered onto the top of the boat's navigation lights and stood there, teetering. The children had him cornered.

"Just grab him!" Amy ordered. "Grab him with your *hands*!"

Brogden tried his best to stay balanced, but the boat's swaying made it difficult. He stole a nervous glance at the water below. Whereas only a few minutes before he'd been in awe of the lake's beauty, the waves were choppy now, and an ominous mix of blue and gray. Looking at it him sick to his stomach, and he was sweating with fear.

"I've got him!" Emory cackled triumphantly.

Brogden saw the hands closing in on him and did the only thing he could think of—he turned and ran. Unfortunately, he ran into nothing but air!

Worse still, Emory's hands caught a piece of him, and for a brief moment Brogden was positive that his leg would be ripped off!

But no! Emory only succeeded in tearing his little shoe away.

"My shoe!" Brogden cried as he tumbled through the air.

"Did you get him? Did you get the little man?" Amy asked.

Emory turned and held up the little shoe. "No, just this!"

"Give it to me!" Amy commanded, and for a moment they struggled, tugging the shoe back forth.

Brogden, meanwhile, had plunged deep into the cold water, and for the second time that day he worried that he would drown. Even in the midst of his terror, however, he managed to marvel at the way the light sparkled as it filtered through the water, which was as green as a forest of pines. He opened his mouth to call for help, and it quickly filled with water.

What was it that Aunt Gladys had told him about swimming? He tried desperately to remember. *Kick?* Yes—kick! That was it! He kicked furiously with both legs and flapped his arms in a pulling motion. At first, nothing happened. Then—*oh thank heavens!*—Brogden began to move upward! Up and up and up! His lungs were straining and his ears were plugged, but he didn't let up. He kicked and pulled until the light above his head grew brighter and the water became clearer. Then, all of a sudden, his head popped through the surface! He gasped for every bit of air he could pull into his lungs.

"There! There he is!"

Brogden looked up and saw that Emory was leaning over the edge of the boat with the net, aiming it at the water now. Amy stood at his side, directing.

Brogden kicked with all his might even as the net splashed down next to him. Water sprayed into his face, and he sputtered as it went in his mouth and up his nose. He managed to paddle a few feet away, but the net came down again. It was only a matter of time before Emory would scoop him up, he realized. His long, wet hair was slowing him down, and the more he kicked, the more tired his muscles became. How he wished he'd been more diligent about doing his morning calisthenics, which Aunt Gladys insisted upon. ("Healthy body, healthy mind!" she sang out each morning at dawn.) If only he was stronger, he thought, he could hold out much longer. But his kicks slowed, and it felt as though he was treading through mud.

Relentlessly the net slapped onto the water again and again, searching and scooping, searching and scooping.

"Do you have him yet?" he heard Amy ask over and over.

"Naw!" Emory yelled back.

"Let me try!" Amy cried. She ripped the net out of Emory's hands.

Brogden felt his final bit of energy drain away. He was completely worn out now and couldn't summon another kick or stroke of his hand.

The last thing he remembered seeing before he slipped under the waves was a gigantic beak heading straight toward him!

CHAPTER 6

Brogden is Left Behind on Sunset Island

Brogden felt a sharp prick near the small of his back and realized in horror that he was being lifted by the seat of his pants! His dripping body came away from the water with a slurping sound as he was carried into the air!

"*Aaahhhh!*" he screamed.

He was dangling from the beak of a brilliant white heron! Brogden didn't known this yet, however, because his long hair was hanging down in front of him. All he could see through the wet strands were the waves of the lake beneath him, which became smaller and smaller as the bird flapped its wings and rose higher and higher.

Brogden could still see Emory and Amy. They continued fighting over his tiny shoe. But gradually, the boat and the people on it became tiny specks as Brogden was taken further away.

He figured out pretty quickly that he must be in a bird's beak because he could he could hear wings making powerful shushing sounds. And when he looked up, sure enough, he saw its beautiful feathers. In spite of the horror he was feeling, he told himself not to squirm. He most definitely did not want to fall back to the lake from such a great height, and that would mean almost certain death!

Brogden's seasickness aboard *Almost Home* was nothing compared to how he felt zooming along through in the air. The bird (and he selfishly hoped it was an eagle or a falcon, because at least that would be something impressive to tell Aunt Hazel...) flew around the outside of the lake, banking and gliding dangerously close to the trees! For no apparent reason and without warning, it would alternately swoop high and low, which made Brogden feel quite ill, so he decided it was best to keep his eyes closed. (And he prayed that he wasn't being taken to a nest.)

Suddenly, the heron dove downward at alarming speed! Brogden managed to wipe his hair aside just in time to see a small island ahead of them. The bird seemed to be heading straight for it. At first it looked like a weird green blob. But as they approached it, the green came into focus, and the island became a cluster of treetops and bushes with one solitary house. Down, down, down the bird flew at a precarious speed, and Brogden feared that perhaps it planned to drop him at some point. He braced himself for the inevitable crash as he scanned the island for a soft landing spot.

Then he felt a tremendous change in air pressure as the bird's wings stopped beating, and they began gliding instead. Below, a grassy patch rose quickly toward them.. The bird continued its smooth descent and fluttered its wings twice more before fanning them out. Then, at last, they came to a halt.

Before he could say "Let me go!" Brogden was released from the bird's beak. He tumbled onto the soft green quite shaken and dizzy and remained there for a long time, gripping fistfuls of grass and breathing heavily.

The bird used its beak to prod him—his sides, his shoulders, his hair.... It wasn't painful, and it didn't seem as though the bird wanted to harm him. If anything, it only seemed to be investigating him. When the bird's beak poked at the soles of Brogden's feet, he burst into a fit of giggles because it tickled so much. Then, even though there was still some fear flowing through him, he rolled over to properly meet the creature that had rescued him from a horrible, drowning death in Lake Wahkmo.

His gaze was met by a long, pointy, orangey beak which ended near the heron's tiny eyes. Its face was neither gray nor white nor black, but a stunning blend of all three, with a tinge of blue mixed in. Its neck, which was mostly white underneath and a smoky gray on top, seemed to stretch on forever. The bird's massive grayish-blue wings were now tucked tightly against its body, which was held up by two legs that reminded Brogden of skinny twigs. Although he had hoped the bird had been an eagle, he wasn't disappointed. This heron, he thought, was just as magnificent.

"Wow!" Brogden breathed as he stared. Then, remembering his manners, he exclaimed as sincerely as possible, "Thank you for rescuing me!"

The heron cocked his head to one side as if considering the words.

"Thank you!" Brogden repeated. "I don't know what I what I would have done without you! I owe you my—"

"Not a fish!" the heron squawked. "Not a fish!"

With a toss of its majestic beak, the heron turned away and rose mightily into the sky. A cool breeze ruffled Brogden's hair as the bird's wings began beating for takeoff. He got to his feet and watched it soar away.

"My life!" Brogden cried out. "I owe you my *life*!"

The heron stretched its wings out fully, banked to the left, and flew off. Brogden watched until it was just a tiny speck against the clouds.

The flight and the flapping had dried Brogden's clothes, and his hair was only slightly damp now. Invigorated and hungrier than ever, he realized he needed to find something to eat. He tried to ignore the fact that he was even farther from home than ever. Once he had eaten something, he'd come up with a plan to get off the island and head back. At least that's what he told himself.

He got a good look at the island's layout when he was in the air. There was a single house right in the center. Several paths ran away from it in different directions and ended at small beaches on either side. He also saw a mixture of colors on the western part of the island: white, pink, purple, yellow.... He assumed that they were masses of flower blossoms, and blossoms could only mean one thing—*berries*. They might not all be ripe yet, but at least they'd be *something*.

He paused for a moment and watched his shadow stretch away from his body. It was a trick Aunt Hazel had taught him so that he would be able to get his bearings.

After studying the shadow's position for a moment, he headed west through the grass.

About ten feet on, Brogden came to a bush with dark green, waxy, oval-shaped leaves. The edges of the leaves curved up and inward. Brogden recognized it as a 'Drinking Bush,' which Aunt Hazel had taught him to identify when he was only four or five years old. She had said it was a plant that could save someone's life! Sure enough, when he gently pulled one of the leaves off, he found a sizeable amount of water sitting in the middle of it. He raised it to his lips and drank gratefully. His stomach thanked him with a rumbled that also reminded him solid food would be appreciated even more.

He continued westward until the land sloped downward. The grass gave way to a rocky path, which he followed for quite some time. Then he came upon three cherry trees whose white blossoms covered the ground. Brogden approached the first tree and studied its bark. There didn't appear to be any decent footholds or branches jutting out, so he moved on to the next tree. Two squirrels were playing a game of 'Round the Trunk,' in which one of the squirrels covers their eyes and counts to five, giving the other squirrel a head start to climb up the tree. The first squirrel goes up the tree after counting and tries to catch the second squirrel's tail. The running and chasing continues up and down the tree, around and around, sometimes for hours. Not wanting to interrupt the fun the squirrels were obviously having, Brogden moved on to the third tree.

This one had several bumpy knots protruding from its trunk, and Brogden was able to climb up to a branch about four or five feet above the ground. It was small, thick, and sturdy, and he rested on it for a moment. It held his weight easily. From there he looked up and was thrilled to see clusters of tiny berries hanging down from branches above.

He dug his toes into more knobby knots and reached up to grab a higher branch. Pulling himself up with both arms, he swung his up wrapped them around the branch until he was hanging like a monkey. Finally, he flipped over onto the top of the branch and sat down. He plucked a handful of berries, and it took all of his willpower to not shove the whole cluster into his mouth at once. But Aunt Gladys' voice popped into his mind—"Proper digestion begins with proper chewing," she always said. So he plucked off the ripest of the berries and bit off small chunks. The taste was terribly sour, but he didn't mind. Within seconds the berry was gone except for the pit. Dropping the pit, he yelled, "Look out below!" He kept this up as he devoured many berries, even those that were so sour they made his lips pucker and eyes squint.

With his belly full, Brogden was now ready to formulate a plan. The branch he was sitting on was still too low to see very far, so he continued climbing higher and higher until he had a better view of the island. To the east was the house, and it didn't look nearly as nice as it had from the air. He could also see three rocky paths which led to the beaches, one being the path he'd just followed. Two docks and a boathouse were also visible, but since he was looking down at them, he couldn't tell how many boats, if any, were inside it.

The boathouse was the most promising thing he'd seen so far. The House Dwellers occupying the crumbly old house would have to leave the island at some point. As soon as they did, he would stow away in their boat and bum a ride to the mainland. *Yes*, he decided, *a boat is definitely the key to getting home.* So he decided to begin the search for one at once.

He shimmied down the tree trunk and walked along the stone path until he came to a beach. There were no boats of any kind there. He strolled across the sand to the water's edge, where a clump of cattails were sprouting up, and clouds of gnats spun upon the water's surface. Below them, the lake was still and green. Large patches of algae spread out in fuzzy, floating masses. But since there were no boats here, he decided to move on.

As he turned to leave, however, he heard voices.

"It's probably just a rumor," said a first one.

"Well, even if it is true, you can't go by appearances alone," said a second.

There was a moment of silence and Brogden wondered if perhaps he'd been mistaken, if it had just been the wind or something. But then he heard them again.

"And anyway, there's no proof of anyone being hurt," said the first voice.

"So far as we know," said the second.

"True, true," agreed the first.

Then there was silence.

Brogden gazed all around but he didn't see a single soul; just a few bubbles breaking on the surface of the water near the cattails. Then he remembered what Aunt Hazel had told him about fish-talk.

"Fish carry on their conversations in bubbles underneath the water," she'd said. "Their words float on up to the surface in the bubbles and then…POP! The bubbles burst, the words drift out into the open air, and anyone in the surrounding area can hear them. That's why you must never tell a fish anything personal. It could become the gossip of the town." (Brogden told her she didn't have to worry. He didn't think he'd ever have the opportunity to talk to a fish, and even if he did, he didn't have any deep, dark secrets that anyone would be interested in knowing anyway.)

This must be fish talk, he thought. He walked closer to the water's edge and waited. Sure enough, more bubbles rose to the surface and popped—and he could hear the fish-words as plain as day!

"Well, what he saw was definitely scary," said the second voice. "A long neck, large body, big tail…. And big teeth, too—lots of them! Definitely not like anything he'd ever seen before in these waters!"

"Water snake," stated the first voice quite confidently.

"Not likely," the second argued. "The body was too big. But whatever it was, I'm not taking any chances. I'm staying on this side of the island."

"I think you're overreacting," the first said. "Until I see something with my own eyes, I refuse to believe that we're in danger here in Lake Wahkmo."

Danger? Brogden repeated in his mind. *Danger???*

He gasped and thought back to the croaking frogs from the night before, and about Amy questioning Varick about a monster in the lake. Could all of these incidents be related? He waited for more bubbles to break, but the water remained still. The fish must have moved on.

A chill ran up and down his spine, and a layer of goosebumps rose on his arms. What if there really was some dangerous creature in the lake? He remembered his jump off the boat and near drowning, and he shuddered. All he wanted now, more than anything he'd ever wanted before, was to get off the island and back to his hut. He would spend the rest of his days, he vowed to himself, staying as far away from Lake Wahkmo as possible!

As if his legs could carry him home right at that moment, he jumped to his feet and ran back down the rocky path the way he'd come, searching desperately for a boat.

The rocky path split both left and right, and Brogden took the path to the left. Just like the other path, it sloped down to a beach. Two kayaks, one blue and one yellow, were drawn up onto it, their paddles strewn beside them as if someone had just used them. Perhaps whoever that was would return soon. *I could probably stow away in a kayak*, Brogden thought.

Close to the kayaks were three large flat rocks. He

climbed onto the largest one and sat down to wait. It was very quiet for a long while; all he could hear was the splashing of small waves as they collided with the shore. Two gulls landed on the beach nearby and pecked curiously at the sand. But finding nothing of interest, they eventually lifted off into the sky.

Waiting was not easy for Brogden. To help the time pass, he played a game that Aunt Hazel had taught him. It involved imagining you were going on a picnic and remembering what to bring. When he and Aunt Hazel played together, they would repeat what the other person had said, then add one more item. This would go on until the list got very long, and one person inevitably made a mistake. Brogden found that it wasn't nearly as much fun playing alone, and by the time he had come up with list of twenty items to remember, whoever had left the footprints still had not returned. Perhaps they were not going to use the kayaks again that day, Brogden reasoned.

As the sun was beginning to sink into the sky, Brogden slid down from the rock. He decided to retrace his steps and try the path that led to the right. This one was quite different from the first two in that it twisted around like a snake. At one point it narrowed considerably, almost disappearing into thick groves of bushes covered with yellow flowers. Being just shy of a foot tall and only a few inches wide, Brogden had no difficulty fitting through. But he imagined House Dwellers would find the path quite challenging.

It sloped downward like the other paths, and he

presumed it would lead to yet another beach. It did indeed, but the final approach was different on this one. It was lined on both sides with black metal torches that were about as tall as Brogden himself. The tops of the torches had small black pots decorated with S-shaped cutouts that would have allowed light to pass through if the candles inside were lit. Brogden stood on his tippy-toes and peered inside one of the pots. It held a small ivory candle as well as few tiny black beetles.

"Neat!" he exclaimed, thinking that it would be fun to walk on the path at nighttime when the torches were lit. He counted the others by twos as he walked past them. Arriving at the beach, he saw that it was the largest of the three and, by the look of it, the one that got the most use. Four white reclining beach chairs faced the water, a blue towel was thrown over the back of one of them. A radio on the sand blared out a song that Brogden had never heard before, but he liked the sound of it. It had a catchy beat and a refrain that went like this:

We're steppin' out,
Steppin' out into the night
Takin' a break
And everything will be alright.

He tapped his feet and hummed along until he realized he was not alone—a tall man was standing on the beach! Thankfully, his back was to Brogden. He had wavy, brown, shoulder-length hair, and he was wearing a wrinkled gray tee shirt and navy blue shorts. He was watching a frizzy haired woman try to maneuver a small sailboat in the water. She seemed to be having a terrible time with it. The boat came to a stop as she adjusted and readjusted the sail. Several times the boat tilted sharply as the sail dipped downward, almost touching the water. The man yelled things like "Jibe!" and "Tack!" to the woman, who looked quite frazzled.

Brogden hid behind a bush with orange bell-shaped flowers and watched the scene with a mixture of interest and dismay. He'd never seen a sailboat up close, but it was obvious even to him that the poor woman didn't know what she was doing at all. (His life would most certainly be in danger if he had to depend on her to transport him off the island! he thought—and just as this occurred to him, the ship's boom swung around and clocked Ms. Frizzy Hair in the head!)

"Concentrate!" hollered the man on the beach, through cupped hands. "You have to get this!"

That's right, thought Brogden. If the frogs and fish and Amy were correct in thinking that there was a dangerous monster in Lake Wahkmo, this woman was going to be its next meal if her sailing skills didn't improve!

"I *am* trying!" Ms. Frizzy Hair called back. "It's not as easy as it looks!"

"Okay, why don't you take a break?" suggested the man on the beach. "You've been at it all afternoon."

Ms. Frizzy Hair needed no further coaxing. Somehow she managed to bring the sailboat to a wobbly resting place on the beach, then she jumped out of it. Beads of sweat dripped from her brow as she made her way unsteadily to one of the beach chairs and collapsed into it.

"Phew!" she breathed. "Does it look like I'm getting any better, John?" she asked.

John walked over and sat down on the chair closest to her. He rested his elbows rested on his knees as he leaned toward her.

"Not really," he admitted. Then in a low voice (which Brogden had to strain to hear) he said, "It's crucial that you learn to sail. You have to, Elaine. Just in case."

"Why are you whispering?" Elaine asked. "No one can hear us out here. There's not a soul on Sunset Island except for you and me and—"

"Sound carries across the water!" John cut her off. "If anyone were to find out…"

"How can anyone find out?" she asked, sounding exasperated.

From the moment he'd hid behind the bush, Brogden's nose itched. Perhaps he was allergic to the bell-shaped flowers. He wasn't sure. All he knew was that the longer he stood here, the itchier his nose got. He rubbed at it furiously with the back of his hand, and then he had to stop to wipe at his eyes because they began to water. And then….

Oh no—

"At-*choo*!" he sneezed. "At-*choo*! At-*choo*!"

John and Elaine looked at each other in astonishment.

"Who's there?" John called out, turning.

Brogden didn't know what to do. His encounter

with House Dwellers in the morning had been less than desirable, and he was unsure if that was how all House Dwellers would react to the sight of him.

I could run back down the path. I could hide in one of the kayaks. I could climb a tree and-

"At-*choo!*"

This sneeze was even louder than the first. No matter what, he knew he couldn't remain under the bush for long.

"Who's there?" John asked again.

"John...do you think...?" Elaine's question hung in the air between them. She reached out and grabbed his arm.

"Stay right here," he said. "I'll go see what it is."

Elaine watched John cautiously as he rose and walked off.

"It sounded like it came from over there," she offered, pointing to the bush with the orange flowers. Brogden knew then that it was too late. He couldn't run, so he had to stay perfectly still and perfectly quiet. The smallest noise, and he'd be—.

"At-*CHOO!!!*"

This was the loudest sneeze yet, and the next thing Brogden knew, a pair of strong hands had parted the leaves and orange flowers.

Now he found himself staring up into one of the friendliest faces he'd ever seen.

CHAPTER 7

JOHN AND ELAINE MAKE BROGDEN
FEEL RIGHT AT HOME

"Well now, who do we have here?" John chuckled. He had twinkling blue eyes with small crow's feet at the corners and a smile that stretched from ear to ear.

Brogden tried to speak. His lips moved, but no words came out.

"That's okay. I know who you are. You're a Foot," John said.

Brogden's eyes widened in disbelief.

"That's right," John continued. "Oh, I know all about the Foots that live in the hills around Lake Wahkmo. My family has told stories about them for years." He laughed heartily. "I just never thought I'd see one here on Sunset Island. And now," he added, "you'll have to bring me to your treasure."

"That's leprechauns. And gnomes," Brogden corrected him.

"Is that so?" John chuckled. "Guess I'll have to find myself a leprechaun then. Or a gnome."

Brogden didn't reply to this. Although John seemed friendly enough, Brogden wasn't sure if he could be trusted.

"Well," John went on, "judging by your eyes and

nose, you must be allergic to Lil' Belle."

"Lil' Belle?"

"That's her name," John said, indicating the bush. "And there's her mama, Big Belle." He pointed to a huge bush a few feet away. That one had even larger orange, bell-shaped flowers. Brogden made a mental note to stay clear of Big Belle.

He leaned forward and studied John close to see if he was being sincere.

"It's okay," John said. "It's perfectly safe out here. Come now, I want to introduce you to Elaine."

Brogden finally emerged from the bush. Although his heart was beating hard with fear, at least his eyes felt a little better.

"Shall I carry you?" asked John.

"Certainly not!" Brogden retorted indignantly. "I can walk!"

"Very well," said John. "Follow me."

They walked across the sand to where Elaine was standing by the beach chair.

"Look who I found hiding behind Lil' Belle," John said, looking down at Brogden with a smile. "A Foot!"

After his encounter with Emory and Amy and their dad, Brogden wasn't sure how Elaine would react. He half-expected her to scream or try to grab him or something. But Elaine was clearly made of stronger stuff. Even if she was alarmed at the sight of him, she didn't show it.

"It is a pleasure to meet you, Mr....um, Mr. Foot," she said. She knelt down next to him and extended her hand for a shake. Brogden decided that her face, like John's, appeared very kind. Her eyes were a soft chestnut brown and framed by long lashes. She had dimples that showed when she smiled. He had never touched a House Dweller's hand before, and when his slipped inside hers, he was surprised at how soft and warm it was. She smelled lovely, like lilacs. He also noticed an unusual but beautiful black and sparkly pendant hanging from a chain around her neck.

"Actually, my name is Brogden," he said shyly.

"Okay," Elaine said. "Tell me how you've come to be on Sunset Island, Brogden."

"I...I was left here by a giant bird," he sputtered, then proceeded to tell her about his home with Aunt Hazel and Aunt Gladys, the encounter with the gnome, and the disastrous drop down the swale. He also told her about waking up in the drainpipe and hurting his ankle.

"You poor thing!" she cried, smoothing down his hair sympathetically. John offered to take a look at his ankle and proceeded to unwrap the bandage. He diagnosed it as probably just a sprain or a badly bruised muscle. There was still a bruise, but hardly any swelling at all.

"You did a fine job with the bandaging," John said as he wrapped it up again.

As they all seated themselves on the lawn chairs— John and Elaine on one and Brogden facing them on the other—Brogden continued telling them about Fred and Nancy and Ollie and about his ride with Dad and Emory and Amy. How he had been called a monster. How he had almost drowned. How he had been pursued by the fishing net.

"How perfectly awful!" Elaine cried, her brow furrowing with anger.

He finished by relating how he'd been lifted into the air by the heron, at which point John broke in with all sorts of questions—How was the view? (Amazing, Brogden exclaimed.) How high do you think you were? (He wasn't sure.) And more until Elaine held up her hand to interrupt.

"I don't think Brogden needs to rehash every single detail from his flying experience in one evening. He's exhausted from the whole traumatic ordeal, John, and needs to rest."

The sun had sunk down below the hills, and in its wake it left a smear of purple, pink and orange across the sky. The three of them could barely see each other in the growing dusk.

"The heron left me on this island, and I've been hoping to stow away in one of your boats and get a ride back to the hills," Brogden said. "Aunt Hazel and Aunt Gladys must be frantic about me."

Elaine suggested that they go inside and have a bite to eat; they could discuss how to get Brogden home over a nice dinner. John agreed that it was a wonderful idea because he was gradually being bitten to death by mosquitoes.

Brogden followed John and Elaine along the path between the torches and onto another path he hadn't seen when he was wandering before. The new path was a mosaic of black, red, and blue tiles. It wound on for a bit, past several trees on each side. Sets of wooden wind chimes hung from their branches and sang out mystical songs; deep and resonant low tones, high tinkling plinks, and mellow chimes mixed together beautifully as the soft lake breezes swirled around them.

"Almost there," Elaine said as they came to a clearing in front of the house. It looked even crumblier now that Brogden was so close to it. The steps that led to the front door were at odd angles, and paint was peeling from every surface. Cobwebs occupied the spaces between the railings that led up the stairs. Moss, branches, and dry leaves hung down in disarray from the gutters, and a tangle of ivy ran up the length of the stone chimney. Brogden craned his head back as he took in all of these details.

"This house and Sunset Island have been in my family for years," John told him. "It was built by my great-grandfather as a retreat from his busy life. When it passed down to my grandfather, I spent many summers here with my brothers and sisters and cousins. We loved exploring the island. My grandfather even built a tree house for all of us. It's still here!" He pointed toward the top of a tree in front of the house, but it was too dark for Brogden to see anything.

"After Gramps died," John went on, "my aunts and uncles wanted to sell the island. Private islands go for a fortune these days you know.". Brogden nodded as if he was used to discussing the price of real estate. "But Elaine and I...well...we needed the house. We had just gotten married, and she just fell in love with it. So the family decided to let us sign a five-year lease."

They came to the front door and John went in. But Brogden hesitated. He had never been inside a House Dweller's home before.

As if she could sense his uncertainty, Elaine flicked on a light and held the door wide open for him.

"Welcome home!" she said cheerily.

Brogden stepped tentatively inside and followed John into a parlor. It had two large floral couches and several comfortable-looking chairs. A brick fireplace was at the far end, and there was a delightful aroma coming from somewhere else in the house.

"Chili," John said, noting that Brogden was inhaling deeply. "We've had it simmering in the crock-pot all day."

Brogden had no idea what a crock-pot was, but he was about to find out. He trailed after John and Elaine into the kitchen. A white wooden table with four matching chairs occupied the center of the room. Two bowls, two glasses, two napkins, and two settings of silverware were arranged on it. Elaine reached up into a cabinet to get another bowl for Brogden.

"Why don't you fetch some pillows, John?" she asked. "Or whatever you can find. A box or something for Brogden to sit on so he can reach."

While he went to look, Elaine lifted the lid off a large ceramic pot, and more of the delicious aroma wafted out. She stirred the contents with a long-handled spoon, then placed some of it into each of the three bowls.

"I don't know if you'll want some shredded cheddar cheese or sour cream on top. We've got both. And these," she laughed, pouring large triangular-shaped chips into a large red bowl. Brogden had never eaten any of these foods, but he didn't want to appear impolite, so he eagerly offered to try them all.

John returned with a black plastic crate and a small, flat pillow. He placed the crate upside down on one of the chairs and the pillow on top of it. Then he helped Brogden climb up to the top of the pillow, which proved to be the perfect height.

Brogden enjoyed the chili immensely: the spiciness of the meat, the stringiness of the melted cheese, and the cool smoothness of the dollop of sour cream were all wonderful. He also relished the crunchiness of the tortilla chips (he ate three of those). Then Elaine cleared the bowls away and brought out a gallon of chocolate chip mint ice cream. She scooped some into three wafer cones, asked Brogden if he wanted sprinkles (he did), and suggested that they sit out on the porch while they ate them.

The air was much cooler outside than it had been earlier, and it was pitch black except for the soft light cast by the moon. They sat on the swings watching the fireflies and eating their ice cream, and Brogden thought it was perhaps the one of the nicest times he'd ever had in his life. Elaine asked some questions about where he lived and about his aunts and his life near the swale, and John promised him that he would take him home the next day. They had a several boats that could get them to the mainland. From there, John said, he'd drive Brogden home.

"But how will you know where I live?" Brogden asked. "The hills around Lake Wahkmo are huge."

"A map," John reassured him. "First thing tomorrow we'll spread out the map and figure out the location of your hut. Don't worry."

The flickering of the fireflies and the steady chirruping of cicadas were making Brogden sleepy. His eyelids began to droop and he had to fight to keep them open.

"Brogden dear," said Elaine gently. "You've had a busy day. It's time to get you to bed. We'll put you up in the guest room."

He didn't need to be asked twice. He allowed Elaine to carry him up the staircase that led to the second floor. (The steps were too high for him to climb on his own anyway.) As they went down the second-floor hallway, he noted that all of the doors were closed.

"That's our room," Elaine said, indicating the door directly across from the staircase. Then she said that, if he needed it, the room next to their bedroom was the bathroom.

She continued down the hallway past another closed door. Brogden wondered what room that was, but since Elaine made no mention of it, he decided not to say anything. When they reached the end of the hallway and the very last door, she turned the knob.

"This is the guest room," she said with a flourish as the door swung back. "For you, our guest!"

Brogden couldn't believe his eyes. It was the most magnificent room he'd seen so far.

"Now, this wasn't always a guest room, mind you."

Brogden turned and found John standing there.

"If you recall," John went on, "I told you that my great-grandfather built this house as a retreat. Well, this was his special room, where he came to get away from everything."

Brogden thought it looked more like a room to get *to* everything. A bay window extended outward, looking out upon Lake Wahkmo. In the moonlight, the surface of the water sparkled like a million diamonds. A telescope stood on the floor by the window, and John explained that it was for seeing the moon and stars and planets. A pair of binoculars hung from a peg to the left of the window, and John said that his great-grandfather used them for watching eagles and hawks. A strange looking rubbery loop hung on the wall to the right.

When he saw Brogden eyeing it, John said, "Ah yes, you might enjoy seeing how Great-Granddad's fish food slingshot works." He reached into a sack on the floor below the loop and took out a handful of brown pellets. He then opened one section of the window before pulling the loop back until it could stretch no further.

"Watch there," he said, pointing to a particular spot on the lake that was bathed in moonlight. He inserted the pellets into the loop and let go. Brogden watched as the pellets flew from the slingshot through the air and across the night sky. As they fell toward the lake, several fish jumped out of the water. Even from this great distance he could see their silver scales glistening as they arced up and caught the pellets in their wide mouths.

"Wow!" Brogden whispered.

While Elaine disappeared to draw the bath water for him, John let him try the slingshot. He marveled each time the fish rose and fell in the moonlight.

"If you think that's amazing, come take a look at these," John said.

A small wooden table in one corner was piled with at least a dozen wooden tubes of varying sizes and colors. He showed Brogden how to lift the tubes to his eye and turn them so that he could see the explosion of colors in symmetrical patterns inside them. John explained that they were called 'kaleidoscopes,' and that each was handmade by his great-grandfather from unique collections of objects that he'd found on the island, such as pebbles and small pieces of colored glass.

The kaleidoscopes weren't the only items that John's great-grandfather had made. John showed Brogden several watercolor paintings, pottery he'd shaped from the island's earth clay, and a small homemade wooden glider that was hanging from the ceiling. There were also glass paperweights with pressed flowers, carved soapstone statues of waterfowl, reed flutes, and a collection of colorful glass animals. Hundreds of maroon-covered books with gold embossed titles stood neatly in cases along an entire wall.

"Bath's ready!" Elaine interrupted. She led Brogden

down to the second of the closed doors, where a claw-footed tub was filled with about six inches of bubbly water.

"I assumed you'd want bubbles," she smiled. "They're so relaxing." She showed him where she had laid out some washcloths, a bar of soap, a small plastic sailboat that she'd found in the attic, and one of John's tee shirts for him to change into.

She closed the door, and for the next half hour Brogden enjoyed the only bubble bath he'd ever had in his life. He floated the boat up and down in the warm sudsy water and scrubbed his skin and hair clean. He felt rejuvenated when he emerged and put on John's tee shirt. It was much too large for him; he had to gather it up in folds and hold it in his hands when he walked so he wouldn't trip. But it had a crisp, cozy feeling that made him feel quite snugly.

"I'm going to give these a wash," Elaine said, gathering up his dirty, smelly clothes when he came out of the bathroom.

"Thank you," Brogden said before letting out an enormous yawn. He followed Elaine back down the hall to the guest room.

The bed stood so high that he couldn't see the top of it; only the checkered quilt that hung down around the sides. He grabbed hold of a corner and, like a mountain climber, used it to scale the mattress. Once on top, he saw that it created the illusion of sitting on a soft, puffy cloud, and he was certain he was going to have pleasant dreams.

Elaine helped him pull the blankets back, and then

he laid his head back on the pillow (which really did feel like a puffy cloud). After she'd pulled the covers up to his chin, John came back into the room, and the two of them sat on the bed smiling at him.

"Would you like a story?" John asked. Brogden said he most definitely would. Aunt Hazel often told him stories before he went to sleep.

"But I'm not going to tell you a story," John said. "I'm going to *read* you a story, out of a book. Okay?"

"Okay," Brogden replied.

Standing in front of the wall of books, John read some of the titles aloud. *Black Beauty*, *Journey to the Center of the Earth*, *Moby Dick*, *Around the World in Eighty Days*, *The Three Musketeers*, *The Wizard of Oz*. These were classics, John explained. They all sounded so interesting that Brogden couldn't decide which one he wanted to hear. He did want something with a good ending, so John suggested *The Wizard of Oz*, telling him about Dorothy trying to find her way back home to Aunt Em and Uncle Henry in Kansas.

To Brogden's pleasant surprise, John was a very expressive reader. He made up all sorts of voices for the characters, which really made the story come alive. Brogden was just a little scared of the Wicked Witch, and was delighted by the Munchkins. Gradually his eyelids began to droop. And as much as he tried to stay awake, he had fallen asleep by the time Dorothy and Toto were on the Yellow Brick Road and meeting the Scarecrow.

John closed the book, and Elaine brushed Brogden's hair away from his eyes. They stood smiling at their unexpected tiny visitor.

"Good night, little Brogden," she whispered. They stood a minute in the doorway, then John flicked off the light and shut the door.

CHAPTER 8

Brogden Investigates a Mysterious Sound in the Middle of the night

Now, although Brogden was so tired, he only slept soundly for the first few hours. A few minutes past midnight he was awakened by a strange humming sound. At first he shrugged it off as some sort of an animal or bird outside. He slid down the quilt and went over to the large window and stood there listening. But the humming noise was *not* coming from outside.

The sound grew louder and louder, and the floor began vibrating underneath his feet. The longer he stood there, the more unnerved he became. He scrambled back into bed, where he tossed and turned for the next five minutes, unable to sleep. The humming sound continued, and he couldn't imagine what it was. But as he was wide awake, he decided finally to get up and investigate.

It was difficult for Brogden to open the door because he was so short, so he took one of the reed flutes and pushed on the doorknob with it. After several minutes of trying he finally managed to get the knob to turn and the door swung open. He padded down the hall to the first room where, peering through the open door, he could see John and Elaine sleeping. He felt somewhat silly and began to reconsider an idea he'd had about waking them up on account of his being scared. He'd just go back to bed and pull the covers over his head, he decided. But as he turned to do so, the humming sound grew louder. It was definitely louder from where he stood in the hallway than it had been in the guest room.

As he made his way back down the hallway, he stopped in front of the door to the second room. It had been firmly shut when they all came upstairs and when he'd been going to and from the bath. But as he passed it this time, he noticed that it was propped open. He pushed on it gingerly with his pointing finger, and it swung open with a creak. Peering through the opening, he was shocked to discover that it wasn't another bedroom as he'd been expecting. He slipped inside quietly to take a closer look.

It was like an office of some sort. There were more shelves of books along one of the walls. However, the books in this room were all sorts of colors and shapes and sizes and were sloppily stacked in no apparent order. A second wall was completely covered in cork. Maps were pinned to it and covered almost all of it. Against the third wall, dozens of white plastic containers were stacked three and four high. One of the containers was partly open. Brogden walked over and stood on tiptoe to peek inside it.

The container was filled with walnut-sized orangey pellets, and he reached inside to feel one of them. It had a powdery feel, and when it broke apart in his fingers it gave off a shrimpy smell. Brogden wondered if John also used these pellets in the fish-food slingshot. And if not, what kind of a creature would eat such things? He hadn't recalled seeing any pets in the rooms downstairs. Maybe the pellets were used as fishing bait.

A single small lamp on the desk cast a soft amber glow throughout the room. Brogden shimmied up the chair leg and climbed onto the top of the desk. It was piled with more books and a hodge-podge of papers. Concealed under one of the papers was a book with a blue leather cover. If he had been able to read, he would have known that it said "Elaine's Journal" on the front. A small gold lock held the pages shut, and Brogden wondered why a book would be secured in this way.

He walked around the top of the desk in search of a key, but stopped in his tracks when he heard footsteps approaching. Quickly, he pulled the top drawer open and crouched down inside it. He wriggled so that the drawer almost closed, then watched through the opening.

It was John. He strode into the room towards the containers. He spoke quietly to himself as he lifted one of them and carried it toward the door.

"Not that I mind, but I hope that our little baby will outgrow these nighttime feedings soon," he muttered. "Then we'll get a decent night's sleep."

Brogden was puzzled.

Little baby?

What little baby?

Just then John's gaze fell upon the desk.

"That's funny," he said, walking over and pushing the desk drawer all the way in. Now Brogden was completely in the dark! He listened intently, and as soon as he was sure John had left the room, he began to wriggle back and forth...back and forth...back and forth...back and forth. Finally the drawer began to open again.

A little more, thought Brogden hopefully. *Just a little more*..., When it was open about an inch, he was able to poke his arm out. This gave him enough leverage to push against the top of the desk and open the drawer a few more inches—enough space to free himself!

He scrambled out, slid down the leg of the desk, and ran off searching for John. Catching sight of the top of John's head descending the staircase, he peeked out through the railings on the landing until he saw John reach the bottom step. Then he started down the stairs himself. Elaine had carried him up the stairs earlier in the evening, and he quickly discovered that getting down them would be quite an ordeal. Standing on the top step, he extended his foot, testing how far it would reach—which wasn't very far, so he could not step down. He then tried jumping with both feet at the same time from one step to the next. However, he realized that if he continued in that manner, it would take him the full night to reach the bottom and he'd never catch up with John. So, although he knew what he was about to do was dangerous, he decided that, in the interest of time, he had no other choice.

Lying on his stomach, he slid down backwards, bumping on each stair (he counted fourteen) as he went all the way to the bottom. By the time he reached the last step, his ribs were so sore that he could barely stand up.

He scouted around for John, who was neither in the

living room nor the dining room, so Brogden moved on to the kitchen. The humming sound was louder than ever, and it seemed as though it was coming from directly beneath him.

He saw nothing unusual in the kitchen and thought maybe John was on the porch. But when he looked a second time, he noticed that a door in the kitchen was open. Upon investigation he found a set of cement stairs leading to the basement. Figuring that must be where John had gone, he jumped onto the first step. There was no way he could slide down the cement stairs on his stomach and still keep his bones intact, so he jumped from one to the next (counting fifteen this time) until he reached the bottom.

In the basement, there was still no sign of John. A single white light bulb hanging above a workbench illuminated a huge freezer, a washer and dryer, and an assortment of old furniture, including an antique hat stand, four chairs with red velvet seats, a grandfather clock whose pendulum was not swinging, and a curio cabinet with a collection of china dolls. The dolls' wide-eyed painted faces stared out blankly at Brogden. Those eerie faces coupled with the humming noise—was even louder now—made him more uneasy than ever. He wanted nothing more than to be back in the bed in the guest room, with the covers up to his chin and his head on the soft pillow.

He turned to climb back up the stairs when, out of the corner of his eye, he spied another open door. It wasn't all that much taller than he was, and it would have been discreetly hidden behind a large wooden bureau except that it looked like someone had pushed the bureau aside to get to it. An open padlock hung from the door, and light streamed through the opening.

Brogden realized the humming sound was definitely coming from behind the door! Even stranger was the fact that the humming sound was actually a 'yumming' sound—*yummmmmm...yummmmmm*. Brogden's curiosity was piqued now; he was determined to find out where exactly the sound was coming from and what was causing it.

Heart pounding, he walked over and pushed the door open. This revealed another staircase, and he started down. The passageway was narrow and the ceiling quite low. It was also drafty and damp, and a cool breeze hit Brogden in the face as he descended. He breathed it in, recognizing it as the smell of lake water. With each downward step, he grew chillier, and the yumming sound grew louder.

With three more steps to go, he was startled to hear another voice—John's—which carried through the air, above the yumming.

"Easy now girl," he heard John say. "There's plenty here. You'll get a bellyache."

With two steps to go, he heard what sounded like a splash, followed by John's laughter.

"You silly! Now I'm soaked through, and these were my only clean pajamas!"

Brogden jumped to the bottom step, which ended at a cinderblock wall. He turned the corner and there was

John. He was standing in front of a huge tank filled with greenish water. Next to John was one of the plastic containers that had been in the second bedroom. John was throwing the orangey pellets into the tank...which then went into the mouth of a large greenish-black monster with...with...

> *a long neck tail..*
> *and fins...*
> *and humps...*
> *and glistening black scales...*
> *and two rows of long...pointy...razor-sharp...teeth!*

Brogden didn't mean to scream—but he couldn't help it.

CHAPTER 9

MAGGIE

John whirled around quickly.

"Brogden! How? How did you ever get down here?"

John rushed over and bent down to put his arms around Brogden's shoulders as he tried to calm him.

"I...I...I followed you down here," Brogden managed to stammer. He couldn't tear his eyes away from the creature. Away from those *teeth*.

"Oh, dear. We didn't mean for you to see, for you to find out," John said softly. "We wouldn't ever want you to be frightened. You see, Maggie here," he pointed with his thumb to the creature swimming in the tank, "is our little....well...our *big* secret."

"I'll say," Brogden agreed and he stole another shy look at the creature. She was making the yumming noise, and it sounded like it was coming from her throat.

"Why...why is she making that noise?" Brogden asked.

"She's telling us that she loves her midnight snack, just like you enjoyed the chili," replied John. "Would you like to feed her?"

"I...I guess so," Brogden said, his eyes wide with uncertainty. John reached into the container and handed one of the pellets to him. He then picked up Brogden and held him near the top of the tank so that he could toss it over. Maggie's body swirled around in the water, but her alert and sparkling eyes never left the pellet. It plunked into the water with a splash, and before it could even begin to sink, Maggie's wide mouth closed around it—and again Brogden glimpsed the ferocious-looking rows of teeth.

"Yummmmmm. Yummmmmmmm," Maggie crooned while she chewed.

Brogden continued tossing the pellets into the tank, and Maggie eagerly snatched each one until the container had just a few crumbs at the bottom. Then she looked searchingly from Brogden to John, hoping for more.

"That's all there is, girl," John told her. "You'll have to wait until breakfast."

With that, Maggie lowered her eyelids, and Brogden could see that they were fringed with long lashes. She flipped over and floated on her back, full and content.

Brogden looked up at John, his mind reeling with questions. Then they started tumbling out like a rushing waterfall—

"Who is she? Why is she here? How did she get here? Is she the monster that all of the lake creatures are talking about? The one that the frogs and fish are afraid of? Is she dangerous?"

"Whoa there, little Brogden," John laughed, holding up his hand to halt the interrogation.

"I'll tell you everything about Maggie. But first, come over here...."

There was a small bench in front of the tank, and John motioned for Brogden to sit down. He then turned one the empty container upside down and sat on top of it so they were facing each other. Despite the early hour, Brogden felt more awake and alive than he ever had in his life.

"First off, you are not in danger. You have my word," John began. "But Maggie is. Or was."

"What do you mean?" Brogden asked. Maggie had begun to snore in a gentle low rumble as she continued floating on the water's surface.

"You see, Maggie's mother is named Morag. She lives in Loch Morar in Scotland. For years people have been trying to capture her. Those same people would do anything to get their hands on Maggie," John began.

"What would they do to her if they captured her?" Brogden asked.

"If that ever happened—and I am hoping that it never does—she could be put on display in an aquarium or..." John paused for a moment and his face darkened. "She would be studied in a lab and..." He looked as though he wanted to say something else, but decided against it. "Let's just say that there are plenty of greedy folks who'd love to have Maggie's head hanging on their wall, or her teeth strung on a necklace. Plenty of folks who'd do anything for a little bit of fame and a pile of money."

Both of them sat quietly mulling over his words, and for a few minutes all that could be heard were Maggie's snores.

"Elaine belongs to a very special group of people," John went on.

"Scientists?" guessed Brogden.

"No. Conservationists of Unusual Creatures of the Sea, or 'COUCS.' Some people call them KOOKS. They think they're crazy in the head. But nothing could be further from the truth. Elaine was a marine biology major in college. That means she studied the lives of animals that live in the seas and oceans. She was at the top of her class. But she wasn't satisfied with just studying whales or dolphins," he said.

"That's right, Brogden," interjected a voice.

John and Brogden turned around. Elaine was standing there in a fuzzy bathrobe and slippers.

"You see, when I was seven years old, my family rented a house near a lagoon by the Chesapeake Bay for the summer. The backyard sloped down to the lagoon, and a wooden dock stuck out into the water. I was allowed to play on the dock as long as I didn't go too close to the edge," she said.

Brogden smiled. It reminded him of the swale.

"Every morning I'd go outside into the backyard and sit on the dock," she continued, "and watch the boats going by in the lagoon on their way to the bay. Mostly small fishing and crabbing boats. I would stand on the dock and wave to the fishermen."

Again Brogden thought of the swale and of all of the things that floated by in its waters, and of the red-capped gnome in the basket-canoe.

"Well, one day I was sitting cross-legged out near the end of the dock reading a book. It was my favorite place to read. And as I was turning a page of the book—which was a 'Nancy Drew' mystery by the way—I noticed something out of the corner of my eye. It was two blackish humps sticking up out of the surface of the water. I set down my book and stared because I wasn't sure what it was. Maybe it had just been the light playing tricks on the water. But no—all of a sudden a dark brown head rose out of the water! It was kind of small and looked like the head of a snake. I watched as its eyes moved slowly about, looking left and right. After a few moments the head rose higher into the air, and I could see that it was attached to a very long neck. Maybe two or three feet! Well, I must have coughed or made some sort of a noise, I can't remember exactly. All I know is that the creature turned and looked directly at me."

Brogden's eyes were wide with astonishment. He couldn't think of anything to say.

"I think it's important to mention here that I was pretty much a tomboy when I was growing up," Elaine pointed out. "My mother had four boys before I came along, and when she finally had a daughter, she couldn't wait to put me in frilly dresses and buy me dolls to play with. But I wanted none of that. I loved nothing more than hanging around my older brothers and climbing trees, collecting bugs and worms, and watching birds from our tree fort. And reading, of course. Growing up with only brothers turned me into a pretty tough cookie. I've had more frogs put in my bed and spiders hidden in my hair than I can count," she said. "So when that creature rose out of the water and looked straight at me, I wasn't afraid at all! Quite the contrary. I just looked at it calmly and called out a hello to it," Elaine said.

"Wow!" breathed Brogden, impressed.

Maggie was still floating happily in the tank. Her snoring had ceased and she was now humming a tune in her sleep. It had a hauntingly beautiful sound.

"The creature swam over to me and introduced herself," Elaine went on. "Chessie, that was her name. She informed me that she normally lived out in the bay, but that she had to keep on the move because fishermen were always trying to catch her with nets or hooks. She had been on the run from them when she had gotten disoriented during the change in tides and wandered into the lagoon."

"She was friendly?" asked Brogden. "She didn't try to harm you?"

"Goodness no!" Elaine laughed. "Chessie was glad to have some conversation! She hung around under our dock for about a week. Each day I would sit out there and tell her all about my brothers, and she told me all about her cousins: Nessie and Morag who lived in Scotland, Champ who lived in Lake Champlain, and Ogopogo who lived in Lake Okanagan. She said that they were all terribly misunderstood by humans. who assumed that they were ferocious beasts." Elaine shook her head sadly at this.

"And then what?" Brogden asked.

"This part is disturbing," John warned him. Then,

to Elaine, "He may be too young to hear it."

"I am not! I'm thirteen!" Brogden pleaded. "Please, tell me what happened!"

Elaine studied him intently. Perhaps she was thinking of everything Brogden had told her about his adventures, falling down the swale and how brave he'd been. In any case, she nodded solemnly.

"Okay then. So, I was saying how Chessie had been visiting with me by the dock for about a week. Some days she'd tell me stories about the different kinds of sea creatures—mermen, mermaids, kraken. Some days she'd just float nearby while I read my books. It was the most magical feeling, you know, having her there close to me. It was late in the evening, around dusk, on the day everything went wrong. I had been tossing chunks of leftover chicken from dinner to Chessie and she was showing off her long neck as she caught them. And then, do you remember I told you about the fishermen who traveled up and down the lagoon? Well, a small crabbing boat was making its return trip up the lagoon toward us, but Chessie and I were so engrossed in our game that we didn't notice until it was about ten or twenty feet away, and by then it was too late." Deep lines crossed Elaine's forehead as she recalled these events.

"One of the men on the boat had spotted Chessie and alerted the others, yelling that there was a monster in the lagoon. Within seconds they were upon her, casting out their lines. Some of the men were leaning over the side of their boat, frantically trying to grab at her with their nets, with their hands—anything. A few of them actually jumped overboard and swam toward her with long-handled knives!"

Brogden sat in silent shock.

"Chessie dove deep and took off," she went on. "That was the last time I ever saw her. And when she was gone, the water was littered with poles and nets and long-handled knives."

"Elaine has made it her life's work through COUCS to protect creatures like Chessie from the ruthless people who want to harm them," John said. "A few months ago, COUCS got wind of the fact that Morag was about to give birth to a baby in Loch Morar," he said.

"Maggie?" Brogden guessed.

"Yes," he said, nodding. "Unfortunately, the MHS had found out, too."

"MHS?" Brogden repeated, confused.

"Morag Hunting Society," John explained. "A group of people who spend their days chasing Morag so relentlessly that she rarely sees the light of day. They stood ready on the shores of Loch Morar with binoculars, guns, nets, and who knows what else."

"Why didn't you ask the police for help?" asked Brogden. He knew about the police. Sometimes he heard their sirens, and Aunt Gladys had explained that they were brave House Dwellers who helped keep other House Dwellers safe. You could always go to the police for help in an emergency, she'd told him.

"We tried," John said.

"But not all people believe in sea creatures like Chessie and Morag and Maggie," Elaine cut in. "When we went to the police, they told us to stop wasting their time with such foolishness, and that they had real crimes to deal with. So, to make a long story short, we rescued Maggie ourselves. As soon as she was born, we took her on a long boat ride."

"In a special water-compartment," John continued.

"And then flew her in a plane," Elaine went on.

"In a special water-container," John added.

"And then drove her here," said Elaine.

"In a special water-truck," John said. "And then came the hardest part."

"Other than separating her from her mother," Elaine pointed out. "That was awful for both of them, but Morag understood that it was the only hope for a peaceful life for her baby."

"Yes of course," John agreed. "Other than that. So, we had to unload her from the water-truck under cover of darkness. We put a leash around her neck, which she didn't like at all, lowered her into Lake Wahkmo, and sailed here to Sunset Island. Maggie swam beside us. Because she had been kept in such small spaces for weeks, it was hard to hold onto her. All she wanted to do was dive and dip and twirl."

"The sailboat almost capsized several times," Elaine remembered with a smile. "John was trying to hold onto Maggie while I maneuvered the boat. And as you could see yesterday, I'm not the greatest sailor. I never have been."

"How did Maggie get in here?" he asked, gesturing toward the tank. "How does the tank work?"

John rose and motioned for Brogden to look at it more closely.

"See that thing?" he asked, pointing toward the back. It was hard, with the water being so murky, but Brogden could see a tall metal grate; an expanse of crossed silver bars. "The spaces in the grate allow the lake water to pass through. And when you press this button"—he pointed to a black button on the wall next to the tank— "the grate lifts up so that Maggie can swim freely in Lake Wahkmo. She needs the exercise, and she loves being free for awhile. Of course, we didn't let her do this right away. We wanted to make sure that she'd return to us first."

"Lake Wahkmo is a safe lake, and Maggie can grow up here without the fear of being hunted," Elaine finished. "Mostly because no one knows she's here."

Brogden didn't want to upset them, but he felt it was the responsible thing to let them know that what Elaine had just said wasn't entirely true. He told them about the frogs and the fish-talk and Amy's conversation with Varick. He speculated that although House Dwellers didn't know Maggie was in Lake Wahkmo, she had definitely been seen (probably when she was outside the tank), and that word was spreading like wildfire among the lake's water creatures that a dangerous, monstrous creature was on the loose.

"Well they're not in danger at all!" Elaine said indignantly. "Maggie wouldn't hurt anyone...or anything,

Despite her fearsome looks, she is a very gentle creature. *She's* the one who needs protection."

They sat quietly for a moment then, watching Maggie trilling softly, each deep in their own thoughts. Brogden wished that Aunt Hazel was with him right now, seeing and learning all about Maggie.

"We can continue this conversation in the morning," John said. "Let's head upstairs. Like Maggie, we all need to get some sleep."

"Agreed," Elaine said, and off they all went.

CHAPTER 10

JOHN HELPS BROGDEN FIND HIS WAY BACK HOME

Brogden slept fitfully in the guest room. In his dreams, he was sitting next to the tank singing a song while Maggie turned somersaults in the water. With every flip and swish of her tail, Maggie would smile, and Brogden would reward her with the orangey shrimpy-smelling pellets. He wasn't a foot tall in this dream—he was the same height as John, so it was easy for him to reach over the top of the tank and feed Maggie right out of the palm of his hand. John and Elaine, meanwhile, were floating around the tank in their sailboat. John was eating an enormous ice cream cone with sour cream on top, and they were both smiling and laughing.

Then the dream abruptly changed. A giant frog appeared in the tank, croaking "Danger! Danger!" Dozens of fish of all kinds surrounded Maggie with bubbles coming out of their mouths. The bubbles rose to the surface, and as they popped, all Brogden could hear was, "Monster! Monster!" Poor Maggie became paralyzed as the fish surrounded her, moving in closer and closer. Her eyes sought out Brogden's through the tank's window, imploring him to help her. But the more she needed him, the shorter he shrank. He was forced to watch helplessly as fishermen with nets and poles and long-handled knives banged on the grate, shouting "Get her! Get her!"

"What should we do?" Elaine and John called to him.

Brogden looked around. He had nothing to defend Maggie with. The only thing in the room was a white plastic container, and when he opened it, he was dismayed to see that it was filled with more sour cream.

"How?" he cried out.

"Throw the sour cream! Throw the sour cream!" John and Elaine screamed together.

Brogden grabbed the container, but knew he was too short to throw it over into the tank. He couldn't reach!

"Throw it! Throw it!" They were all chanting this— John and Elaine, Maggie, the frog, the fish, even the fishermen. The heron reappeared, soaring above them, with its giant beak opening and closing as it squawked, "Brogden! Throw the sour cream!"

"I can't!" Brogden sobbed. "I can't!"

A pair of hands was shaking him gently as a voice called to him.

"It's just a dream, Brogden! It's just a dream!"

He opened his eyes to find John and Elaine standing over him, their faces filled with concern. For a moment, he couldn't remember where he was. Sunlight was streaming through the window. He blinked his eyes several times and gazed slowly around. Then it all came flooding back to him. He was in a house on Sunset Island, in the middle of Lake Wahkmo, and a magnificent sea creature named Maggie was swimming in a tank in a secret room below the basement!

"Good morning, sleepyhead!" John smiled, tousling Brogden's long hair.

Brogden felt embarrassed when he realized that they had probably heard him cry out in his sleep.

"Yes, I…I was having a bad dream," he said sheepishly. "Is Maggie okay?"

"She's better than okay," Elaine reassured him. "In fact, she's already eaten her breakfast. Would you like to see her after you've eaten yours?"

Brogden couldn't think of anything else he'd rather do, and he said exactly this. Elaine disappeared for a moment, then returned with a gleaming silver tray. It held a plate stacked high with steaming slices of a yellowy looking bread, a tall and frosty glass of orange juice, and a fresh napkin. He thought everything looked and smelled delicious and was eager to try another new House Dweller food.

"French toast," announced Elaine. "I think you'll like it with butter and syrup. I know I always do."

"Oh, thank you," Brogden replied, touched by their kindness. He'd never had breakfast in bed before.

Sure enough, he did like the food. The butter had melted into golden pools between the slices, and Elaine poured warm syrup over the whole stack before cutting the slices into bite-size pieces. The combination of the melting butter and the warm syrup filled his tummy, and he found he liked it even better than the chili and ice cream from the night before. The outside of the French toast was crispy and the inside was soft and squishy, and he savored each bite.

Elaine and John sat at the foot of his bed watching contentedly while Brogden ate. He was enjoying it so much that he said very little...just chewed and swallowed...chewed and swallowed.

He polished off the final piece of French toast and drained the orange juice from the glass, tipping it back until it was empty. Then, without meaning to, he let out a ripping great burp.

"Excuse me," Brogden apologized, blushing, even though John and Elaine were laughing out loud. "It was all just so delicious." He dabbed at his mouth with the napkin.

"It's quite all right," Elaine said. "I'm glad you enjoyed it. Would you care for some more?"

"No, thank you." Brogden patted his tummy. "I'm so full!" Secretly he was thinking that if he spent any more time eating with these House Dwellers, perhaps he'd grow to more than a foot tall! "Can we go and see Maggie now?"

"Oh, I think Maggie would enjoy that!" John said.

"But first things first," Elaine cut in, handing Brogden his own clothes, which she had washed and dried. They smelled clean and fresh and slightly lemony. John and Elaine left him to change. After he emerged in the hallway, they headed down to see Maggie.

John offered to carry Brogden down the staircase, and the ache in his ribs from his late-night slides convinced him to accept the offer. The basement didn't seem half as ominous as it had in the middle of the night. John set him down in front of the tiny door behind the bureau while he removed a key that hung from a black cord around his neck.

"I never take it off, except to undo the lock," he told Brogden. "I even sleep with it. There is only one other key to this room and it's hidden."

The lock clicked open and the door swung aside on its hinges. The lake smell (cool and fishy) greeted them as John hunkered down to get through the low opening. Brogden, on the other hand, stepped through easily, then followed John down the stairs to the room with the tank.

Maggie was swimming in circles underneath the water, her undulations creating waves that looked like a string of hills and valleys. But when she heard them approaching she swam up the front of the tank, lifted her head, and flashed a toothy grin. Although John had said Maggie was harmless, Brogden was still awed by the sight of her. Her scales, her tail, her teeth....

John reached into his pocket and pulled out a small green pellet.

"Here you go. Toss this in," he said, handing it to Brogden.

"What is it?" Brogden asked, turning it over in between his fingers. He brought it to his nose and sniffed. It didn't smell like the other pellets.

"A vitamin," John said. "Because Maggie is not growing up in Loch Morar, she is missing some of the nutrients that she would normally get from the plants there.

This vitamin is made from plants in Loch Morar."

Brogden threw the pellet high into the air and over the top of the tank, and in a wink Maggie snatched it up. She looked inquisitively at John as if to ask if there were any more.

"That's it for today, Maggie girl," he said. Then, to Brogden, "Too many of those can make her homesick for Loch Morar and Morag."

"Will she ever be able to return to Loch Morar?" Brogden asked. "Will she ever be able to see Morag again?"

He and John sat down together on the bench and watched Maggie swim.

"Maybe in time," John said. "Right now she can't defend herself against predators. And if Morag was slowed down because she was trying to protect Maggie, we'd run the possibility of losing both of them." Then he added, "For now, this is the only solution."

Brogden thought about how he was like Maggie, how they were both far from home. And sensing this, John put his hand lightly on his shoulder.

"As much as we would love to have you stay here as our guest for a few days—you know, as a sort of holiday—we should think about getting you home. I'm sure your aunts will be so glad to see you."

Maggie slithered along the bottom of the tank and blew bubbles through her large nostrils.

"You'll always be welcome here," John added.

Brogden smiled and nodded in agreement. If he didn't believe that his aunts weren't crying their eyes out right now, he would have no problem staying on for a few days. But the sooner he was able to let them know he was safe and sound, the better.

Then he said what had been on his mind since his conversation with John and Elaine in the middle of the night.

"You can trust me, you know," Brogden said earnestly. "I swear, I won't tell anyone about Maggie being here." He paused. "Ever."

"Why, I never thought you would," replied John. "Now say a goodbye to Maggie, and we'll go look at my maps to see if we can figure out where you belong."

Brogden walked up to the tank, and Maggie swam over to see him. Their faces were very close, separated only by the glass. He raised his hand to wave, and Maggie raised her tail. It plopped down with a mighty splash and drenched the top of Brogden's head. He laughed heartily and shook his hair from side to side, flinging the water droplets everywhere.

"Goodbye Maggie," he whispered softly. "I wish I could stay here longer and get to know you. But…well…you see, I have to get back to my home by the swale. I have to let my aunts know that I'm safe. And *you* stay safe, too, Maggie," he choked. "Maybe someday I'll come back and…" His words trailed off. He stared hard at her, trying to memorize exactly what she looked like; the length of her neck, the curves of her back, the way the light played upon her scales. He felt certain that, as long as he lived, he would never witness such an incredible creature again. She gazed back at him, then lowered her lashes and swam off toward the back of the tank where she began turning somersaults. Brogden stole one last look at her before turning away and starting up the stairs behind John.

Back up in the second room, John spread a map of Lake Wahkmo across the desk. Brogden climbed up and knelt down next to the map. John explained how a map gave you a bird's-eye view of the lake and the hills that surrounded it. Brogden thought he'd had his fill of bird's-eye views for awhile! The map of Lake Wahkmo was strikingly similar to the view he'd had when he'd been dangling from the heron's beak. He preferred a map, he told John, because it made him much less queasy.

John pointed out the little picture of the compass rose in one corner, which showed the cardinal directions and the scale that helped you figure out relative size and distance. With a pencil, he drew an 'X' to show where they were on Sunset Island. Brogden learned that there were two other islands in Lake Wahkmo, but they were at the other end of the lake and much smaller. He realized there were symbols for so many other things on the map, too—roads, the marina, the beaches, the docks. And, dotted throughout the hills surrounding the lake, he saw that there were more houses than he had ever imagined. Somewhere under the wooden steps that led to one of those houses was his hut and his aunts!

"Now all we have to do is figure out where your home is," John said, turning the pencil over and over in his fingers as he studied everything.

"It's next to a swale," Brogden offered eagerly, wanting to be helpful.

"That's right, you did mention that," John said. "And that's a fine starting point. But here's the problem." He pointed to the symbol for a swale on the map, which was a thick blue line. Brogden saw John's brow fill with anxious creases, but he didn't need to be told what was wrong. What a fool he'd been to think that his swale was so special, that it was the only one in Lake Wahkmo. As he looked down upon the map, his head starting swimming with dizziness—there were no less than about *fifty* thick blue lines running down hills into Lake Wahkmo! How would they ever know which swale was his?

"They help to move water off the hills and away from the houses," John explained. Then he launched into a detailed explanation of things like water infiltration and runoff and drainage. Brogden listened attentively, and it became clearer than ever how he wound up in the drainpipe.

"The bottom line," John concluded as he folded the map up, "is that, despite the large number of blue lines, we will get you home. I promise you. We'll drive around Lake Wahkmo and search near every single swale if we have to. Don't worry!"

Brogden thought he heard a slight hesitation in John's voice, but he looked at him confidently when their eyes met.

"I'm not worried," Brogden said, knowing it was a little white lie. But he didn't want to hurt John's feelings.

"You two better get a start then," Elaine told them. She was standing by the doorway with a small basket in her hand. "This is for you, Brogden. I made some extra slices of French toast for you to take home. I thought that maybe your aunts would enjoy it." She pulled some items out of the front pocket of her jeans. "I'd like you to have these as well."

The first was a small photo of John and Elaine. In it they were seated on a large rock, and they were both smiling.

"To remember us," she explained.

The second item was a small pair of soft brown moccasins!

"How did you ever....?" Brogden gasped excitedly. They were the most handsome shoes he'd ever seen!

"A few months ago, before we brought Maggie here, my sister came to visit with her family. These belonged to her youngest boy, Nate, who was only a few months old. She must have missed them when she was packing up. I offered to mail them back to her, but she said not to bother because his feet would quickly outgrow them already, and maybe we could use them if we ever had a child of our own someday. I thought you might like them," she said.

Did he ever! Brogden slipped his feet inside and wiggled his toes around. They were lined with some sort of fuzzy stuff that acted as a soft cushion. And they fit perfectly, as though they had been custom made for him! He beamed from ear to ear and could scarcely keep his eyes off them.

"Thank you!" he said, reaching up and hugging Elaine around her neck.

"You're very welcome. And this," she went on after he sat back down, "is a special gift from Maggie."

She pulled a tiny silver chain from her pocket, which she told him was really one of her bracelets, but she thought it would fit him just fine. A glittering greenish-black scale dangled from it, sparkling in all directions as he shifted it from side to side in his palm.

"She sheds them from time to time," Elaine explained as she helped him to fasten it around his neck.

"I will never forget you. Or John. Or Maggie," Brogden said.

Elaine took both of his tiny hands in hers.

"Nor I you," she replied, and Brogden thought he saw tears gleaming in her eyes.

And then, all too soon, it was time to leave. The three walked together down to the beach where the kayaks sat.

"We'll row across to the mainland," John told Brogden. "We own a little patch of land there, and that's where we keep our jeep."

"Jeep?" Brogden squeaked. "Jeep!?"

"It's the best way to get up and down the hills of Lake Wahkmo!" John laughed.

"I've never been in a jeep or a car or anything like that! Wait 'til Aunt Hazel hears about this!" He was suddenly more excited than ever. "Does it go very fast?"

"In her younger days she did," replied John. "Ella Jane—that's the jeep's name—and I used to go for long rides down winding roads, cranking' the music up, lettin' out one gear after another, accelerating faster and faster...." John's face had a dreamy, faraway look.

"Now, that's enough of that kind of talk," Elaine admonished him. "No racing around in the jeep. Take it easy. I mean it. We want Brogden to get home in one piece."

"Right, of course," said John. "Well...we're off then."

He pulled the yellow kayak down the beach to the water's edge, so it was half in and half out. He sat down in it and pulled Brogden on top of his knees.

"Now all we need is a good wave to wash us out," John said.

They sat there, waiting. Twice, small waves crept up the beach and underneath them, but the kayak only budged a few inches. Then, from out in the lake they could see a strong wave, a giant ripple of energy which grew larger and taller as it approached them.

"This is it!" John called to him. "Hang on!"

As the wash of the wave flowed onto the beach, it lifted the kayak up. And as it receded, they were carried out and away from Sunset Island. Brogden held onto the sides of John's knees and stared straight ahead as John began paddling first left and then right. The paddle made gentle splashing sounds each time it dipped into the water. Brogden turned back to wave to Elaine, who was standing on one of the flat rocks. She waved back. With each stroke she grew smaller and smaller. He was torn between looking back at her and watching where they were going. After a while, he turned to wave to her again, but she was no longer in sight.

Halfway between the island and the mainland, Brogden noticed a blurry gray shape, low in the sky. It was advancing toward them quickly and looked like a giant flapping bird. A shiver of fear traveled down his spine and he gripped John's knee tighter. He had no desire to be snatched up by another winged creature.

"It's okay Brogden," John reassured him. "It's only the seagulls, and I know exactly how to handle them."

As the shape grew closer, Brogden could see that it wasn't one giant bird—it was many birds. There were dozens of flapping wings, which did nothing to quell the uneasy feeling he had in the pit of his stomach.

"They're only interested in one thing," John told him. He laid the paddle across the kayak and reached under the seat to retrieve a small bag. "And that's food," he said. He ripped open the bag, grabbed a handful of potato chips, and handed some to Brogden.

"When they get close, start throwing these toward them. You'll see, they'll catch them in midair. It's actually fun to watch. But when we're out of chips, be sure to yell this Promise Poem in as loud a voice as you can—"

> *There are no more*
> *Now go away*
> *I'll feed you all*

Another day!

"And be forceful or they'll never leave!" John told him. "They're very bossy and it's the only command they'll listen to! Get ready...here they come!"

John barely had time to finish barking out these instructions before the birds descended upon them in a flurry.

"Throw!" John yelled. "Throw!"

Brogden threw the potato chips into the air, and the gulls snatched them up seconds after they were released. There were at least twenty of the greedy birds in the frenzied bunch, scooping and snapping their orange beaks.

"More! More!" they screeched.

However, in what seemed like only seconds, Brogden was out of chips. There were only crumbs left in the bottom of John's bag.

"I haven't any more!" cried Brogden.

"What's the promise?" the largest of the gulls demanded, zooming in front of his face, his beak almost touching Brogden's nose. Brogden screamed out the Promise Poem. Instantly the gulls did an about-face and flew off.

"Keep the promise!" the gulls squawked over and over until they were out of sight. "Keep the promise!"

Quite shaken, Brogden shut his eyes and exhaled deeply. He was relieved that he and John encountered no other birds on the remainder of the ride and was quite happy when they drew close to the mainland.

When the kayak got close enough to shore that it

scraped along the bottom, John jumped out. He set Brogden onto the kayak's seat and waded through the water, dragging the kayak behind him and up onto the land. There was no beach; just grass where a black, slightly battered jeep sat waiting.

Brogden jumped out and followed John up to the jeep. It had no doors, so he was able to scramble onto the passenger's seat. John reached over to pull a thick gray strap across his chest.

"Buckle up for safety!" said John as the seat belt clicked shut. After taking a quick look at the map, he turned the key in the ignition. The jeep shook violently and a thundering sound erupted from behind them.

"Needs a muffler!" John yelled over the ear-splitting noise. "But otherwise she runs like a charm!" He shifted into gear, and they jolted forward violently. Brogden was glad he was belted in!

"I figure we'll start here!" John hollered, pointing to the map. "There's definitely a swale running down that hill!"

Brogden nodded to him, then gripped the seatbelt as the jeep lurched forward again. He found himself pressed back against the seat as they climbed upward. They leveled off for a few seconds, then shifted from side to side as the jeep careened down a winding road. With each turn, Brogden hung onto the seatbelt for dear life. During one particularly sharp turn, John glanced over just in time to see Brogden's entire body flying up into the air. Although Brogden's hands were clenching the seatbelt, it looked like he was about to go right out of the jeep! John made a quick grab for him and brought the car to a screeching halt. Brogden's face had turned a sickly green.

"Sorry!" apologized John, muttering something about weight distribution and centrifugal force.

"Too…fast…." Brogden said weakly. "I feel sort of…sick."

"Wait! I know what the problem is!" John exclaimed. "You are getting carsick because you can't see out of the window." He hopped out of the jeep and went around to the back looking for something that Brogden could sit on. He returned holding a can labeled 'Green Latex Paint' and set it on top of the passenger's seat. Brogden climbed onto it. Now he was able to see out the front window, and John pulled the seatbelt over him again.

"I'll slow it down," he promised.

The jeep jumped forward again, and Brogden could see that they were on a road lined with droopy, hairy willow trees.

"I live near a willow tree," he offered.

John pulled the map from the dashboard, opened it, and squinted. "Well, if this map is accurate and up-to-date, there actually is a swale nearby," he said. "Just…around…this…bend…yes…there!"

He slowed the jeep and pulled to the side of the road. After unbuckling Brogden, he raised him onto his shoulder and began walking through long grass. After a few minutes of searching they heard a soft rushing sound.

"There!" cried John "There's a swale!"

It was a swale indeed, with a gentle trickle of water flowing through it. It wound itself down the hill like a giant snake, and as they followed its banks, they looked about in all directions.

"Aunt Hazel! Aunt Gladys!" Brogden called out as they journeyed, just in case they were out looking for him.

They continued on that way—pulling branches aside and calling out for Aunt Hazel and Aunt Gladys—until they reached the bottom of the swale, where it emptied out into the lake. They hadn't seen Brogden's hut. The only person they'd run into was a tiny wood fairy with purplish wings who'd fluttered over to them and kindly asked them to not shout so loudly, as her babies were taking their map.

"I'm afraid this isn't the right swale," John said.

Brogden said nothing. He felt foolish thinking that they would have found his home on the first try.

"Don't worry," said John. "We're just not having beginner's luck is all."

They began making their back up the swale. Brogden worried that he was a burden, riding on John's shoulder. He offered to walk, but John wouldn't hear of it.

"No offense, but we can make better time with my longer strides," John reasoned. Back in the jeep, they looked over the map again.

"Give me an idea of some of the other landmarks," John said. "In addition to the swale being near a willow tree."

Brogden thought hard.

"Well, the wooden staircase leads to a brown House Dweller's house," he said.

"It's a start," John admitted. "Swale...willow...brown house...wooden stairs.... About how far down the hill?"

Brogden wasn't sure. Being only a foot tall, he'd never even been aware of how far above the lake his house was. And having been unconscious when he'd been washed down the swale, he had no recollection of how far he'd traveled.

They tried three more swales on different parts of the lake, beginning at the tops of the hills, parking the jeep, and following the meandering waterways down to the lake. Each time, they kept their eyes peeled for brown houses while Brogden called out loudly for his aunts. They did spy more than a dozen brown houses, many with wooden staircases, but they weren't the right ones. After the fourth trip down and back up again, Brogden felt quite discouraged and worried that they would never find his home.

"Let's stay positive," John said encouragingly when they were sitting in the jeep to rest. "I know! Let's eat the French toast that Elaine packed. We'll need the sustenance if we're going to get you home before sunset."

The French toast was cold and a little soggy, but still very tasty. While he chewed away, Brogden racked his brain for more clues that would lead them to his hut.

"A street address?" John asked, but Brogden didn't know.

"Cars?" Brogden also didn't know.

"Any stores close by?" *I have no idea*, Brogden said again, growing more and more embarrassed.

"The beach where the drainpipe was…did it have a name?"

"I…I.…"

John laughed and ruffled his hair. "Right—you don't know. No problem, we'll figure it out."

They spent the rest of the day in much the same way, driving around the lake up to the top of the hills…locating the swales…following them down…calling out for Aunt Hazel and Aunt Gladys…and having absolutely no luck.

Late in the day, when they were back in the jeep for what seem like the hundredth time with the map spread out in front of them, Brogden realized there were only one or two swales left that they hadn't investigated.

"What if…" he began. But he couldn't bear to finish his question.

"Listen Brogden," said John. His face was kind and earnest, and he took Brogden's tiny hands in his own. "If—and I only mean if we haven't searched for days, weeks, or months even, and if we haven't put out flyers and a search team—if we *still* can't find your home and your aunts…well…Elaine and I have never had any children. I know I'm speaking for both of us. We'd be glad to adopt you, to have you as our son, to call you our own."

Speechless with gratitude, Brogden thought hard about John's offer. He thought of his time on Sunset Island, the mouth-watering food, the cozy bed, John and

Elaine's friendship, and Maggie. What he wouldn't give to live with Maggie every day, to help take care of her, to maybe even train her to do tricks! But then he thought again of his aunts...Aunt Gladys's lessons and chores...his long walks with Aunt Hazel...learning about bugs and butterflies and flora and fauna...watching the boats from Balanced Rock....

"That's it!" he cried suddenly.

"What?" John asked in mild shock. "What's it?"

"Balanced Rock!" Brogden burst out excitedly. "I live near Balanced Rock! You can walk to it from our hut!"

"Well, why didn't you say so?" John threw his head back, laughing joyously. "Everyone knows about Balanced Rock!"

In a flash, Brogden was once again buckled in his 'seat' on top of the paint can, and John was driving at breakneck speed to the far side of the lake, which was much farther away than any spot they had tried all day.

The jeep swerved from side to side, and Brogden held onto the seatbelt tighter than ever, until at last the jeep screeched to a stop. Beside the road, a narrow trough sloped down the hill. A small trickle of water was flowing inside it. John grabbed the map and triumphantly pointed to one of the two remaining blue lines.

"Balanced Rock is halfway down this swale!" he shouted exuberantly. "This must be it! Brogden, I think you're almost home!"

He lifted Brogden to his shoulders and practically ran down the hill, following the twists and turns of the swale, past long grasses and groves of tall mushrooms and clumps of wildflowers. Brogden called out for his aunts once again while scanning the landscape. They passed a maple tree with such speed and enthusiasm that they almost missed seeing a tiny wooden door and the small bearded gnome carrying an axe that popped out from behind it. In fact, if Brogden hadn't been looking down at that exact moment, John might have stepped on the pocket-sized fellow.

"Who goes there?" demanded the gnome, looking up to gaze at them. He raised his axe menacingly.

Cupping his hands around his mouth, Brogden called down, "It's me, Brogden!"

The gnome dropped his axe in surprise. It narrowly missed John's toes.

"Brogden you say?" he called back. "Oh, happy day! Oh, stars and sunshine! Brogden, my boy, your aunts have been worried sick about you! The deer and the squirrels and the chipmunks and the butterflies and the bees have been looking everywhere for you!"

Brogden's heart sank at the thought of everyone being so crazed with worry. "I'm not surprised," he said wearily. "I'm sorry!"

"You'd best get on home, boy," the gnome went on. "They have the mourning torches lit." Then he asked, "Who's the giant?"

"He's a House Dweller named John," Brogden replied. "And he's my friend! He's been helping me find my way home."

"Ah yes," the gnome said. "Well, it's always good to have friends." Then he motioned for them to continue on their way down the swale.

That's when they heard the voices.

"Brogden! Brogden! Brooooooodeeeeeeeennnnnnnnnnnn!"

Louder and louder.

Closer and closer.

"Let me down, John!" cried Brogden. "Please!"

John set him down quickly but gently on the bank of the swale. Brogden ran on, his feet practically dancing in front of him. He couldn't keep up with them.

"Brooooooooogdeeeeeeennnnnnnnnnnn!"

"Aunt Hazel! Aunt Gladys! I'm here! I'm right here!" he called.

John followed behind him. And then he saw it all— the giant willow, the brown house, the wooden staircase, and the teeny hut. The hut was surrounded by dozens of flaming torches no bigger than matchsticks. And in front of it stood two gray-haired ladies, each of them no taller than a foot.

"Aunt Hazel! Aunt Gladys!" Brogden called to them. Their faces registered shock, disbelief, and then joy. They rushed toward him with outstretched arms.

"It's me!" he cried, rushing into their embrace. "I'm here! I'm home!"

"Oh, it's our boy!" Aunt Gladys sobbed, tears spilling down her cheeks. "Look Hazel, our boy's come back to us!"

The three held each other for what seemed like hours. The aunts covered him with kisses and murmured "Thank goodness!" and "Our prayers are answered!" over and over.

Finally they separated, and Aunt Hazel held him at arm's length.

"Let us see you dear," she said. "Are you okay? Where have you been? How did you get home?"

"I want you to meet someone," Brogden began. "He's been my rescuer, my friend, and like…well, like a father to me." He turned to introduce them to John, but at some point in the midst of their reunion, John had disappeared.

CHAPTER 11

BROGDEN DISCOVERS THAT THE REAL DANGER IS CLOSE TO HOME

With each passing day, Brogden's adventure faded a little more, and seemed to grow more distant. Upon his return, the mourning torches had been promptly extinguished and a celebration held. Aunt Gladys brought out a jug of her best honeysuckle juice (which was only for very special occasions) and quickly whipped up a cherry-covered pine-cone pie. Aunt Hazel delivered a most eloquent speech in which she thanked all of the neighborhood creatures who'd taken part in the search. And of course, Brogden's good friend, John, who had played a pivotal role in bringing their boy back to them. All of the creatures were eager to meet John, but Brogden explained that he had already set off on his long journey back to his home on Sunset Island.

The chipmunks, deer, raccoons, squirrels, butterflies, and a few gnomes gathered around while Brogden told the story of his journey. Seeing as the tale was going to last long into the night, Aunt Hazel bribed a dozen fireflies with a jar of freshly collected nectar and they agreed to stick around, twinkling on and off throughout the evening. It was altogether very festive.

Brogden began with his attempt to rescue the

gnome (and asked had anyone had heard of his fate, but apparently he was still missing) and his tumble down the swale. He told them about his friends Fred and Nancy, of his night in *Almost Home*, and all about Ollie. ("I know the family! So many kids!" remarked a raccoon.) He continued with how he had taken a ride in a boat ("Oh, how wonderful!" exclaimed Aunt Hazel) and how he had nearly drowned ("Foolish House Dwellers!" scoffed Aunt Gladys. "Imagine them calling Brogden a monster!"). He told them about his flight in the heron's beak, and how he was deposited onto Sunset Island. (One of the deer shyly asked what an island was, and Brogden had to take at least five minutes explaining.) He described Elaine's scrumptious chili, and the sour cream, and French toast, and John's kayak, and the jeep. He apologized to his aunts for losing his shoes and then displayed his new moccasins, which everyone *oohed* and *aahed* over. Keeping his word, he left out absolutely everything about Maggie. He talked and talked until only Aunt Hazel, Aunt Gladys, and the nocturnal animals were still awake.

"Time to get Brogden safe and sound into his own bed," Aunt Gladys announced when Brogden had finally finished. He fell asleep at once, glad to be home.

In the days that followed, life settled quickly back into its usual rhythm. There were chores to be done, of course. And, like always, Brogden was warned not to go near the swale. (*As if I'd want to go through that again!* he thought.) But he found that while he was sweeping out the hut with Aunt Gladys or helping Aunt Hazel gather stalks of white coral bells for a table centerpiece, his mind drifted away. In comparison to when he was away, his life back at home seemed dreadfully dull. Several times a day, he'd stop what he was doing to wonder what John and Elaine and Maggie were doing on Sunset Island. His aunts noticed the change in him as he became more distracted and day-dreamy.

"Brogden misses his new friends," Aunt Hazel remarked one afternoon when they spied him walking near the rock wall. He was watching the leaves float by in the swale. "He's bored with us old ladies."

"Stuff and nonsense, sister," Aunt Gladys snorted. "He always loved living here with us before. It's that blasted swale. I always knew nothing good would come of it. I'll tell you what he needs—he needs to keep busy. And we've got plenty to do around here, that's for sure."

"But he's seen more of the world now," Aunt Hazel said softly. "Maybe tomorrow I'll take him on a short trip to Wishing Meadow. That's sure to cheer him up."

"After chores, of course," Aunt Gladys reminded her.

"Of course, Gladys," sighed Aunt Hazel.
****

Going to Wishing Meadow—a beautiful expanse of dandelions as far as the eye could see—was a treat usually reserved for his birthday. On previous trips, Brogden always wished that his parents would return. But this time, before he blew the silvery seeds into the wind, he closed his eyes and made different wishes. He made a wish for

Maggie, that she would stay safe from hunters. He wished that he could visit John and Elaine again and spend time with them and hear how *The Wizard of Oz* turned out. He wished that he could make his aunts understand that although he was grateful to be home, in his heart he longed to be in two places at once. He wished for things they would never understand, like the thrill of hanging from a heron's beak and the magic of fish jumping in the moonlight. And although Aunt Gladys would never allow it, he wished for more adventures, too. He walked through Wishing Meadow, from one dandelion to another, closing his eyes and puffing out one wish after another. By the time he was finished wishing, he was out of breath and covered in feathery seeds. They clung to his clothes and stuck in his long hair.

When Aunt Hazel saw him, she burst into laughter.

"Well, if your wishes don't come true, you can't say you didn't try," she chuckled.

Brogden felt bad. It wasn't that he didn't love his aunts, his home, and everything else that was familiar. He just couldn't help thinking back to Maggie and her glistening scales. When he thought of her, he would reach for the scale hanging from the silver chain and rub it between his thumb and forefinger, as if that somehow brought him closer to her. His aunts were curious about the scale, but Brogden said it was just something sparkly that he'd found on the ground.

And then one day, about a month after he'd returned home, something very unexpected happened.

Early in the morning, a large truck came rattling down the steep driveway of the brown house, and if Brogden could have read the words on the side of it he would have known that it said 'MOVING VAN'. He watched from underneath the wooden staircase as two men took many different boxes and all kinds of furniture out of the truck and carried them into the brown house. By midmorning the truck was completely empty, and the two men stood outside, leaning against the truck and thirstily drinking glasses of water. Brogden could hear the clinking of the ice cubes in the glasses.

The larger of the two movers, a burly man with bulging muscles and hardly any hair on the top of his head, wiped his sweaty brow with the back of his hand.

"Glad that's over and done with, Simp," he grunted.

Simp, a shorter and skinnier fellow with floppy dark hair, pointy glasses, and a peculiar mole on his cheek, tilted his glass back and quickly drained it.

"Me too, Macky," he agreed. "And beginning tomorrow we've got to get started on our *real* work."

"You positive this is the right place?" Macky asked.

"My contacts were quite specific," Simp answered. "Lake Wahkmo. From the looks of things, it's smaller than I'd reckoned. Shouldn't be hard to find the little monster."

Monster? Brogden thought.

Monster?!

Goosebumps popped out all over Brogden's arms and legs. His scalp began to tingle, and even his hair stood on end. It seemed impossible, yet Brogden couldn't help wondering if they were talking about Maggie. He continued listening, his ears straining to catch every word that Simp was saying.

"I figure we'll find us a boat tomorrow and get out on the lake. Then it'll only be a matter of time before we track er' down." He glanced around nervously. "Hey, you don't think anyone can hear us, do you?"

"Nah," Macky shook his head. "I'm pretty sure we're the only folks that know or care that the loch baby is here." A grin spread across his face. "And if all goes well, she won't be here long!" His laugh was a wicked-sounding cackle. "You hear anything back from the lab or the aquarium?"

"At the least, both of em' have held firm with their offers. At least one million dollars for her capture," grinned Simp. "Let em' battle it out, I say. Highest bidder gets the nasty, scaly beast!"

"And we'll be rich!" Macky proclaimed.

"Don't forget famous!" added Simp.

The men strode up the front steps of the brown house and disappeared inside. Brogden stood there, dumbstruck, with one thought running like a low rumble of thunder through his mind.

Maggie's in danger...Maggie's in danger....

It seemed too incredible to be true—starting tomorrow, those terrible men were going to be in a boat on Lake Wahkmo hunting for Maggie. And it wouldn't take long for them to find her, since Lake Wahkmo wasn't all that large. And when they did find her…Brogden shuddered at the thought.

In that instant, he knew what he had to do.

****

He spent the afternoon walking around in front of the hut, collecting large sticks. It pleased Aunt Gladys greatly.

"Nice to see you helping to keep our property clean," she noted. "Tidiness is so important."

When he had counted the sticks and was satisfied with the number, he consulted Aunt Hazel about the art of tying knots.

"Well now, what kind of a knot are you interested in?" she asked. "There are all kinds of knots, you know. The square knot, the half-hitch, the figure eight, the bowline." She rattled off at least a dozen more. He finally decided on the timber hitch, and Aunt Gladys tossed him a ball of twine. "Practice with this," she said.

Out of sight of his aunts' prying eyes, he knotted the sticks together with the twine, one next to the other, until he had assembled a wide platform. When he felt confident that it was solid, he dragged it down to the bank of the swale. And it was there, for a fleeting moment, that he began to doubt himself. Perhaps the men weren't after Maggie after all. Maybe they were hunting for some large fish or an eel or a ferocious snapping turtle. It was possible that he had misunderstood them, of course. So he had to be sure Maggie was really their target. Before he put his plan into motion there couldn't be even a shadow of a doubt.

Covering the raft with large green leaves, he left it hidden by the swale and crept back under the stairs. He could hear Aunt Gladys talking inside the hut as she set the table for early dinner.

"Be a dear and call Brogden inside, will you sister?" she asked Aunt Hazel. "He'll need to wash up before we eat, what with all that puttering around he's been doing this afternoon. I don't suppose you have any idea of what he's up to?"

"Not at all, only something with knots," said Aunt Hazel. "Just a moment, dear, I must finish pressing this flower."

Brogden realized that this was his only chance, before his aunts came looking for him and it was too late.

He slipped across the long grass and stood in front of the brown house. The lights were on inside but the curtains were drawn, so it was impossible to see anything except the dark silhouettes of Macky and Simp, who were in the front room. The windows were slightly open, but from Brogden's place in the grass it was hard to make out what they were saying. Even if he went up the front steps, he still wouldn't be close enough to hear.

Thinking quickly, his gaze fell upon the long metal gutter that ran vertically from the roof to ground next to the front window. *It's worth a try*, Brogden told himself.

Aunt Hazel had taught him how to climb trees when he was very young, so he was able to shimmy up the gutter quite easily by holding on with his knees, reaching up, and pulling up with his arms, then grabbing on with his knees again, and so on. Inch by inch he scooted upward until he was eye level with the open window. He held on tight, suspended perhaps ten feet above the ground (and didn't dare look down, for that would make him dizzy). A small breeze fluttered by, and for a brief moment the curtain blew aside and Brogden got a grim view of the two men.

Macky was standing in the middle of the room polishing some sort of a harpoon. The blade flashed in the light. And Simp was loading several dull, brassy bullets into a rifle. Brogden gasped aloud and almost lost his grip!

"Hey! Did you hear something?" Macky asked, his eyes darting nervously from side to side.

"Naw," Simp said, loading another bullet into the rifle.

"I'm sure I did," Macky insisted. "I'm going to check it out."

From where he hung on the gutter, Brogden watched in fear as Macky crossed the room and opened the front door. Brogden held his breath and concentrated on remaining as still as possible while Macky looked left to right...left to right.... Seeing no one, he went back inside.

"Well?" Simp asked.

"Nobody's there," Macky admitted. "It must be my nerves. I won't be able to relax until we've got the little monster."

Simp patted the rifle and smiled an evil grin.

"Tomorrow's a big day," he said. "We oughta get

some rest. And Macky?"

"Yeah?"

"Just in case you have trouble falling asleep tonight, count dollar bills. Stacks and stacks of crisp, green, dollar bills." He cackled and held up something in front of Macky's face. Brogden couldn't see what it was. He leaned in closer toward the window.

"Take a good long look at this picture, Macky," he whispered. "Remember, tomorrow our lives change. Tomorrow she's ours."

Just then another breeze drew the curtain aside, and Brogden could see what Simp was holding. It was a photo, and there was no mistake—*it was Maggie.*

Brogden had to resist the urge to jump all the way to the ground below. He let go with his knees and, holding onto the gutter with only his hands, slid down as quickly as he could. His hands were on fire by the time he reached the bottom, but he had no time to pay them any mind. His legs propelled him through the grass toward the door of his hut. Without pausing, he burst through it, panting breathlessly.

His aunts were seated at the table and, by the looks of things, had been waiting for him.

"Brogden!" Aunt Gladys scolded. "What have we said about banging doors? And go wash up, it's time to eat!"

"No—no time!" he choked out.

"There's always enough time to wash up," Aunt Gladys retorted. "Who knows what germs—?"

"It's okay, Brogden, we don't mind waiting," Aunt

Hazel interjected.

"You don't understand!" he shouted. "I've got to go!"

"Go?" both aunts cried. "Go where?"

"Back down the swale!" he called out over his shoulder.

He flew out the door without shutting it and made a beeline for the spot near the bank of the swale where the raft was hidden. His aunts stared at him as he left, unaware of what he had just said, while the door swung freely on its hinges, creaking softly. And then, as if they'd been hit by lightning, both women jumped up from the table, toppling glasses and dishes as they scrambled out.

"*No, Brogden, no!!!*" they shrieked.

Luckily for Brogden, there were a few inches of water flowing in the swale. When he eased the raft in, it floated easily. He hopped on, and it began drifting along in the slight current. Both aunts had caught up and were running along the bank of the swale, pleading with him.

"Don't go, Brogden! We can't bear it! Please stop!" they pleaded.

"I've got to save Maggie!" he called back.

The raft was picking up speed, and his aunts had to run even faster to keep up with him.

"Who's Maggie?" Aunt Hazel yelled.

"She's a loch monster, but…not a mean monster, she just *looks* like a monster! She's nice and friendly and she's living in a tank in John and Elaine's house on Sunset Island, but these evil men have found out that she's here in

Lake Wahkmo and they want to capture her and put her in an aquarium or a laboratory or worse! She's in the most terrible danger, and I have to warn them!" He spilled out the words as fast as he could because the raft was only a few feet from the drop-off.

"I'll be back! I promise!" he reassured his aunts. The two women were huffing and puffing as they struggled to keep up.

And then his aunts did something that he'd never anticipated when he'd set his plan in motion. Just as the raft was about to plunge over the drop, he felt it shudder as both aunts leaped from the bank of the swale and landed beside him!

"We're coming with you, Brogden," Aunt Hazel stated firmly as the raft flew over the drop.

CHAPTER 12

Brogden's Request is Considered

Although the second ride down the swale was a rough one, the raft proved quite seaworthy, and there was plenty of room on it for the three of them. The two women held on tight as it traveled along, and Brogden took the job of steering with an oar he had fashioned from a stick. He used it to shove off each time they bumped into the sides of the swale. Thankfully, the current was nowhere near as ferocious as it had been during Brogden's first journey, so the ride was fairly pleasant,

"Oh look! Look, dear!" Aunt Hazel pointed out beautiful flowers and plants as they sailed by. "This is splendid! Great fun!" she exclaimed.

"Sister, please do hold on!" cautioned Aunt Gladys, whose face had turned white as a ghost.

Brogden didn't dare speak the worries that were nagging at him as they moved along in the stream. What if they were moving too quickly when they reached the bottom of the swale? What if they couldn't stop when they reached the drainpipe? What if they just flew out into the lake? They'd drown! And it would be all his fault!

"Sensational!" cried Aunt Hazel.

"Hold on!" insisted Aunt Gladys.

"We should have done this years ago!" whooped

Aunt Hazel.

"Hold on!" pleaded Aunt Gladys.

"Wheeeeeeeee!" squealed Aunt Gladys.

"Sister, please!" Aunt Gladys scolded.

"Oh look, dear! Up ahead!" Aunt Hazel pointed to a round opening straight ahead of them. "A tunnel!"

But it wasn't a tunnel at all—it was the drainpipe. And as they entered its darkness, the raft showed no sign of slowing down. On the contrary, it was gaining momentum as it neared the exit.

Brogden saw the circle of light at the other end and made a decision. With just inches to spare, he grabbed hold of both of his aunts' hands and yanked them off the raft, which continued sailing along and out of the pipe. They heard a splash as it dropped into the lake below.

"Wow! What a thrill!" Aunt Hazel declared, leaning against the side of the pipe.

Aunt Gladys had landed on her bum and was soaked. She stood up and sloshed her way through the water to the pipe's opening. She stared wide-eyed at the raft, which was rapidly floating away in Lake Wahkmo.

"Now what?" she demanded. "Now that we are somewhat solidly standing I must say, Sister, that one of us should have remained at home. Must I remind you that our dinner is still on the table? I should have been consulted before you hastily grabbed my hand and pulled me with you into the swale!"

"But dear, look at Brogden," replied Aunt Hazel. She cupped his chin in her hands and stared into his eyes.

"I couldn't bear to let him go alone again. To not know where he was or if he'd ever come back to us." She paused and then winked at Brogden. "And sister, we've never gone on a vacation. It's time we see the world beyond our home!"

"Hmmpf!" snorted Aunt Gladys.

Brogden eyed the water below the drainpipe. This time there was no Frisbee. Scanning the horizon, he did spy two ducks flying in the distance. From far away they looked just like Fred and Nancy! He squinted harder, then let out a whoop of glee....

"Fred! Nancy!" he shouted through cupped hands. "Help! Help!"

The birds continued in their flight, oblivious to his calls. He tried again, louder. Aunt Hazel joined in.

"Yoo-hoo!" she cried. "Fred! Nancy! Over here! This way!"

Aunt Gladys stood resolute, arms folded.

"Silliest thing I've ever heard of, asking ducks for assistance!" she muttered. "What we need is an action plan." She put her hand to her forehead as if to gather her thoughts. "A length of rope and— *AAAAAAAGGGGHHHH!*" she screamed. A water beetle had attached itself to her forehead! "Aagghh! Help me!" she wailed. "Help me!"

Aunt Hazel reached out and deftly plucked the insect away. She held it up to the light of the drainpipe opening, examining it.

"Calm down, Sister. It's just a whirligig. Order

Coleoptera. Family Gyrinidae. Note its feelers, its divided eyes, paddle-like hind legs, and its apple-like scent." She tossed it out of the drainpipe into the lake, where it spun away on the surface of the water. "Most importantly, it's not poisonous at all."

"My nerves, my nerves," Aunt Gladys murmured anyway. "I must sit down a moment."

In the midst of the commotion with the whirligig, no one had noticed that two ducks were hovering in front of the drainpipe.

"Did someone call for help?" one of them asked.

They turned to see where the voice had come from.

"Fred! Nancy!" Brogden exclaimed.

"Brogden?!" Fred was clearly puzzled at seeing him. "Whatever are you doing here...again?"

"Oh, it's a long story," said Brogden. "But we haven't much time to explain. We must get to Sunset Island. It's out in the middle of the lake. Can you give us a float over? I know it's quite far," he said.

"First things first," said Nancy. "Who are these lovely ladies?"

Brogden quickly made the introductions. Each of the women shook Fred and Nancy's webbed feet as they continued hovering. ("Curious! So delightfully curious!" said Aunt Hazel. "A pleasure, Madams," Fred crooned, and bowed his handsome green head before them.)

With the formalities out of the way, Brogden waited for the ducks to respond to his request. They whispered and quacked, their heads close together, as they discussed it.

Finally, Fred spoke up.

"It's not that we don't want to help you and your charming aunts," he said.

"You know we'd do anything for you," Nancy chimed in.

"It's just that...well..." Fred hesitated. "Truth is, we haven't been swimming in the water for quite some time now. We've been spending the majority of our time in the air. You see, we've been hearing from the most reliable sources that a ferocious monster with a very long scaly body and a snakelike head and possibly hundreds, maybe thousands of pointy teeth is swimming in these waters!" He motioned to the lake with his wing.

"It's not safe!" cried Nancy. "All of the lake creatures have been avoiding the water for weeks. Except the poor fish, of course, who have no choice but to stay there. But all of the amphibians have taken to the land, and the birds to the air—"

Brogden cut her off.

"It's not true! Maggie isn't a monster! She looks fierce, but she's no danger to anyone!"

Fred eyed Brogden curiously.

"And you know this...how?" he asked.

"Because...because I've met her!" Brogden sputtered.

"You what?!" Fred and Nancy cried.

"You *what*?!" Aunt Hazel echoed.

They all turned toward Aunt Gladys, expecting her to repeat the question as well, but no such comment came from her.

She had fainted dead away.

CHAPTER 13

BROGDEN AND HIS AUNTS
HEAD TO SUNSET ISLAND
WITH NOT A MINUTE TO LOSE!

It took several minutes for Aunt Gladys to regain consciousness. Nancy fanned her with her wing, and Aunt Hazel gently stroked her arm.

"Come back to us, dear," Aunt Hazel whispered, and at last she did. She looked around, shocked at being in the drainpipe with two ducks hovering nearby, and clasped a hand to her chest.

"My heart…my heart," she said weakly. "And monsters…oh, heavens…."

"Sister, you must pull yourself together," Aunt Hazel told her. "While you were passed out, Brogden told us all about poor Maggie, a victim of unfortunate circumstances and misunderstanding. And whom, as we speak at this very moment, is in grave danger of being hunted by Macky and Simp, two very evil men indeed. But Fred and Nancy, Brogden's fine waterfowl friends, have generously offered to get us to the island where, upon our arrival, we will alert Maggie's caretakers, John and Elaine, of the impending danger. So we must leave at once, and you, sister, need to call upon your inner strength to be brave. Maggie's very life depends on us. Now, will you join us on this rescue mission?"

Aunt Gladys sat stunned, speechless. She looked from Aunt Hazel to Brogden to Fred to Nancy. She looked around at the walls of the drainpipe, as if contemplating other options.

"Quickly, Auntie!" Brogden pleaded. "Time is running out for Maggie! Macky and Simp may be hunting for her right now! We must set off at once!"

Aunt Gladys set her jaw resolutely and nodded.

"I'm in!" she declared.

"Hooray!" cheered the rest, and then it was a flutter of wings as Aunt Gladys and Aunt Hazel climbed aboard Nancy's back. (Aunt Hazel sat in front and Aunt Gladys wrapped her arms around her waist.) Brogden once again sat on Fred's back. Once the passengers were settled, the birds lowered themselves into the water and their webbed feet began paddling.

"Hold tight now!" Nancy instructed them. "Here we go!"

With Fred's feet churning the waves beneath him, Brogden was able to relax a little and collect his thoughts, relieved that his plan was in motion. It seemed a lifetime ago that he had overheard Macky and Simp's plans to capture Maggie. The sun was beginning to set in an explosion of pinks and oranges and he hoped that they would make it to the island before darkness fell.

Meanwhile, Nancy was acting as a tour guide, filling in Aunt Hazel and Aunt Gladys on some of the sights in Lake Wahkmo, including some eagles' nests, a small and twiggy beaver dam, large clumps of lily pads, the grotto of singing frogs ("They're famous for their tenors, you know," she told them), two cascading waterfalls, and an old log filled with seven turtles who had spent the day sunning themselves.

"Marvelous!" Aunt Hazel called out. "Just grand, isn't it, sister?"

"So glad you've cleared up this monster business for us, Brogden," Fred was saying. "I've personally never been a fan of neighborhood gossip."

Brogden glanced nervously at the sky again. *They have to pick up the pace*, he thought.

"No pressure, Fred," he said. "But is it possible to go any faster?"

Fred's green head swiveled around to face him.

"Well, there's always flying," he suggested.

"Let's try it!" Brogden agreed. "Up and away!"

The two birds lifted from the water as their wide wings began beating busily. Brogden glanced sideways at Nancy. Aunt Gladys was quite pale as she gripped Aunt Hazel's waist tighter than ever, but she wasn't complaining. Aunt Hazel was waving to a group of children who were flying kites on the shore. One looked like a red dragon, another like a blue butterfly.

Brogden found himself enjoying the flight; had he not been so worried about Maggie, he would have enjoyed it even more. Fred and Nancy flew much lower and steadier than the heron had (plus he was right-side up this time, not dangling upside-down) and Fred was less slippery than before because he had preened early in the day and most of his oils had worn off. They all made for a graceful picture, what with Brogden's long hair streaming into the wind behind him.

When Sunset Island came into view, Brogden began rattling off directions to Fred. It was truly dusk, with only a slight glow remaining over the western hills. He wanted to be sure to land in the right spot so that they wouldn't have to traipse around the island in the dark.

"Descend slowly please," he instructed, "and circle around There are several beaches on the island, but I'd like to land on the one closest to the house."

"Hold fast then!" Fred called back. He motioned to Nancy, and both birds dipped downward.

"ETA, thirty seconds!" Fred announced. The island seemed to come at them faster and faster. In the dim light, everything looked fuzzy. But as they descended, Brogden could make out the house, the docks, and the kayaks.

"Circle left!" Brogden cried, and as they did he was thrilled to catch sight of John and Elaine. They had just risen from the beach chairs and were heading toward the house.

"Straight down!" Brogden pointed. "There they are!" They went rapidly toward to the beach, and Fred's wings went straight back as he braked against the wind. Brogden closed his eyes as the force almost knocked him off, but he gripped Fred's back tightly with his knees and managed to hang on until they were safely on the sand. He looked over at his aunts and saw that they were already scrambling off Nancy's back.

"Thrilling!" declared Aunt Hazel. "An utterly delightful feeling of being truly alive!" She thanked Nancy with a hug around her skinny brown neck and then helped Aunt Gladys to the ground. Aunt Gladys' hair was sticking out wildly in every direction and her legs were wobbly. She leaned against Aunt Hazel to steady herself.

"Thank you, Nancy," she said with weakly.

"Anytime," Nancy smiled.

Brogden was already running up the beach by this time, shouting.

"John! Elaine! John! Elaine!"

The couple whirled around as Brogden waved wildly to them.

"Ho there!" he called out. "It's me!"

"Quackly!" added Fred, running alongside him.

"I...I can't believe it!" Elaine said. She reached out and grabbed hold of John's arm. "He's come back!"

"Oh my goodness...it *is*!" John replied, his eyes bulging.

The two of them rushed forward, dropped to their knees, and enveloped him in their arms.

"When did you get here?" they asked him. "What are you doing here? And how?" And then, "Oh, how we've missed you!"

Aunt Hazel, Aunt Gladys and Nancy caught up with them.

"Why...who is this?" asked Elaine.

"May I introduce...my Aunt Hazel," he said. Aunt

Hazel curtsied and fluttered her eyelashes.

"My Aunt Gladys," he continued. She extended her hand and Elaine and John gave it a shake.

"It is an honor to meet both of you," Elaine said. "Brogden told us so much about you."

Fred didn't wait to be introduced.

"Name's Fred," he said, stepping forward. "And this is my beautiful wife, Nancy. Not to be presumptuous, but I couldn't help noticing, as we landed, how remote this island is. We've been in the market for a place to settle down, you know, a quiet place, somewhere to start a family—"

"Fred," John cut him off. "Feel free to stay as long as you'd like. I think you'll find it's exactly what you're looking for. By all means, build a nest wherever you'd like. We'd love to have the sound of little ones running—er, I mean *waddling*—around the place."

"Much obliged. Thanks altogether!" beamed Fred. "Well then, if no one minds, I think we'll get right to it!"

"We don't mind at all," John and Elaine said as the others nodded their agreement. And with that, Fred and Nancy lifted their wings in a goodbye and waddled away across the sand.

"John," Brogden started and his tone was serious. "There isn't much time. Something dreadful is about to happen!"

Elaine patted his shoulder.

"Nothing so dreadful that a warm meal wouldn't fix, I'm sure. Let's all go inside and talk over a snack. Your

Aunt Gladys looks like she could use a rest."

Indeed, the flight had not agreed with Aunt Gladys. Her face had taken on a pale green pallor. "I believe some chamomile tea will do the trick," she said.

John and Elaine led them up the beach, past the torches, and into the house. Elaine set Aunt Gladys down on a fluffy couch pillow in the living room and fed her tiny spoonfuls of tea. Gradually the green coloring faded away, although she remained quite pale.

John set two long dishes in front of Aunt Hazel and Brogden.

"Banana splits!" he said with a smile. They were piled high with three flavors of ice cream, wet walnuts, whipped cream, hot fudge, and two cherries each!

"How…how heavenly!" announced Aunt Hazel. Brogden agreed, but his mind wasn't on the food.

"I need to tell you something about Maggie," he began.

"What about her?" Elaine asked. Aunt Gladys had fallen asleep on the pillow beside her, tuckered out from all of the excitement.

"I think—no, I'm *positive*—she's in danger!"

"That's impossible," John replied. "It's safe here. No one would ever suspect that she's in Lake Wahkmo."

But then Elaine touched John's arm gently. "Unfortunately, we can't rule out the possibility that it could be true. Ruthless people will stop at nothing to capture Maggie. Even if it means traveling halfway across the world to track her down. Tell us, Brogden," she said.

"Have you heard something?"

"Worse than that," he said and launched into everything he knew about so far—Macky and Simp's plans, their moving van, the weapons, and the biggest piece of evidence of all, the picture of Maggie that they had.

"This is not good!" John said, banging his fist onto the coffee table. Then he turned to Elaine. "So what do we do about it?"

"We must act quickly," she replied.

From downstairs came the familiar humming sound.

"Okay," John said. "Let's go and feed Maggie and see if we can come up with a plan."

"I'll stay here with Aunt Gladys," Elaine suggested. "I don't want her to be frightened if she wakes up in unfamiliar surroundings."

"Okay," John said. "The rest of us will go, and we'll figure something out."

John carried Brogden in one arm and Aunt Hazel in the other as they made their way down to the basement. As they stood in front of the secret door they could hear splashes.

"*Mmmmmmmmmmm! Mmmmmmmmmm!*"

John removed the key from around his neck and opened the padlock. Brogden had to restrain himself from pushing past him as they descended the staircase; he was so excited to see Maggie again. Aunt Hazel brought up the rear, muttering to herself about how interesting everything was.

When Maggie caught sight of Brogden, she flipped into a series of somersaults before swimming to the front of the tank, where she flashed him a toothy smile.

When Brogden had been back at home with his aunts, he'd often closed his eyes and tried to recall what Maggie had looked like. Now she appeared even more majestic than he remembered. Her scales cast pinpoints of light in all directions, her neck stretched out like a swaying tree, and her powerful muscles rippled as she moved through the water.

"Hullo Maggie!" he said and pressed his face against the glass. Maggie sank below the surface and pressed her nostrils onto the other side. When Brogden blinked, she blinked back. They stayed that way, looking at each other, for a long time.

Meanwhile, Aunt Hazel gasped out a string of adjectives.

"Splendid! Superb! Regal! Dazzling! Such a remarkable, resplendent creature, and right here in our own Lake Wahkmo! Oh, I am so perfectly pleased to be standing here at this very moment! Now I myself have studied flora and fauna for many years, but never have I seen a creature so sublime...so *grand*!"

John pressed one of the orangey pellets into Aunt Hazel's hand.

"Go ahead," he encouraged. "Give her a treat!"

He lifted her high enough to toss it over the top of the tank. Maggie snatched it up in her wide mouth.

"Yummmmmmmmmm!" she hummed appreciatively.

"Yummmmmmmmmm!".

"What a dear," exclaimed Aunt Hazel. "May I give her some more?"

"Of course," replied John. "She'll love that."

He held her up so that she could toss in four more pellets. With each *yummmmmmmm*, Aunt Hazel fell more and more in love with Maggie. To her great delight, after the last pellet was eaten, Maggie performed a series of backward flips and sideways twists. She then glanced shyly at Aunt Hazel, who clapped her hands with glee.

"Bravo, Maggie! Bravo!" she exclaimed, then battered John with a series of non-stop questions—*How old is Maggie? How long is she? How much does she weigh? How many pellets does she eat each day? How often does she exercise?* On and on and on. John answered each one to the best of his ability but explained that Elaine was the real expert.

"I can't believe someone would want to harm her!" Aunt Hazel cried out indignantly. "She's a darling! And she's just a baby!"

"Why don't we discuss this upstairs," John suggested. "You know—not in front of Maggie".

"Oh! Sorry! Of course," Aunt Hazel said.

She and Brogden followed him back up the stairs to the living room, where Elaine sat with books spread out across the coffee table and a small pair of horn-rimmed reading glasses perched on the end of her nose.

Elaine put her finger to her lips and pointed to Aunt Gladys, who was sleeping peacefully and snoring lightly

"I think I've figured out who Macky and Simp are," she whispered. "I've been doing some research." She motioned to the book she'd been reading. Her eyes peered through her glasses as she scanned the page. "Let's see… decades ago, there were two men who were sailing in a boat together in Loch Morar. A creature rose out of the water behind their boat and bumped into the side of it. Says here that the impact was so strong that a kettle of water on the boat fell to the floor. Apparently, one of the men tried to fend the creature off with an oar, and the other fired at it with a rifle. It had to be Morag, Maggie's mother." She paused. "And here…listen to this…it's implied that both men were seen by many as liars. That nobody believed their story, and that they were very bitter about the whole experience."

She continued reading silently for a moment, then looked up and removed her glasses. "My guess is that Macky and Simp are relatives of those men and they are out to prove that their ancestors really did see Morag. One thing really troubles me, too. Those men in that boat assumed that Morag was dangerous when she bumped into them. Did they ever stop to consider the fact it was simply an accident? Or that she might have been lost and was trying to approach them for help?" She shook her head in disgust. "At any rate, Macky and Simp cannot find out where Maggie is. I do believe they mean to harm her!" She put her head in her hands. "What to do…what to do," she murmured anxiously, tapping her nails on the table.

And then Brogden said, "I think I have a plan."

CHAPTER 14

Brogden's Plan is Put in Motion

Everyone was prepared to carry out their part of the plan the next morning. They sat at the table in the kitchen and reviewed it step-by-step during breakfast. Fred and Nancy had flown off at first light. Based on what Brogden had told them, everyone agreed that it was likely that Macky and Simp would be on the move early in the day.

"What can I do?" asked Aunt Gladys. "I want to help." She had slept through the plan-making, which had gone on late into the night. However, she had awakened well rested and determined to make the best of things. Being in the habit of doing morning chores, she had (albeit with some hesitation) helped John feed Maggie her breakfast. To everyone's surprise—including her own—she took an instant liking to Maggie and, like everyone else, was outraged that anyone would want to harm her. So now she wanted to help, but she was having a hard time figuring out how.

Elaine and John looked at each other.

"Well, you could help me with my part," Elaine offered.

Aunt Gladys considered the offer, but shook her head.

"No," she decided. "Too chaotic."

John's eyes lit up.

"You could help me with *my* part," he volunteered.

"Too messy," she said.

"What about helping me, sister?" Aunt Hazel asked.

"I'd rather not," Aunt Gladys replied. "Too painful."

All eyes turned to Brogden.

"Mine?" he asked hopefully.

"No way! Too scary!" she stated and hung her head, disappointment spreading like a storm cloud across her face. "I'm so sorry. I did so want to be helpful."

John slapped the table and everyone jumped.

"Why didn't I think of it before?" he cried. "Come along, Aunt Gladys. I'll show you what you can do!"

"One thing before you go," Elaine said, holding her hand in the center of the table. "All hands in," she said. John, Brogden, and his aunts extended their own hands into the circle until they were piled on top of one another.

"We can do this," she said urgently. "We *have* to do this. Maggie's life is depending on us!"

Everyone nodded in agreement and vowed to do their best.

*****

Brogden guessed correctly—Macky and Simp got an early start. Fred and Nancy spotted them driving a boat away from the marina with Macky at the wheel. Simp was in the rear, fiddling with some unusual-looking instruments.

"How's that thing work?" Fred and Nancy heard Macky say. The two men were traveling up and down the lake, starting along the beachline and then moving further away from it with each pass.

"It detects underwater sound waves," Simp called back. "If that loch baby so much as burps, we'll see it right here on this screen," he chuckled.

"See anything?" Macky asked.

"No, not yet," Simp replied. "But soon. I'm sure of it."

Fred and Nancy kept far enough away so that Macky and Simp wouldn't be suspicious—yet close enough to continue watching them.

****

The sun rose hot, bright, and white when Elaine went outside and pulled the sailboat to the water's edge. She checked that the sail and the lines were in working order.

"I don't think I can do this," she said nervously when John joined her on the beach.

John smiled. "But that's exactly why this part of the plan will work so well," he told her.

****

Aunt Hazel wandered from one beach to another with a jar, searching in the sand. She also looked into treeholes and under clumps of wet leaves as she followed the paths.

"Ow!" she snapped. "That hurt! Ow!"

Aunt Gladys had been right. This part of the plan was painful.

****

Back in the house a short time later, John scavenged through the pantry.

"I know we have more," he said, feeling around for two bags on the middle shelf. Then he reached up to the top one.

"Bingo!" he called out triumphantly.

****

Aunt Gladys sat in front of the secret door that led to Maggie's tank. She spoke through the door to Brogden, who was in the hidden room with Maggie.

"Are you okay, Brogden?" she asked him from time to time.

"Sure am, Auntie," he called back. "Maggie's a quick learner. You?"

"Oh, fine," she said. "But awfully bored."

****

"We're getting quite a workout," Fred declared to Nancy.

"Do you think they've seen us?" she asked him.

"Not a chance," Fred replied.

****

"Do you get the feeling we're being followed?" asked Macky.

"Shhhh!" scolded Simp. His eyes were glued to the needle on the monitor. "I think I just saw something."

"You did?"

Simp studied it intently, watching for anything. Even a little blip.

"No," he concluded. "Nothing. Let's turn er'

around and try the other way."

****

The jar was almost full.

"Just a few more," said Aunt Hazel. She held the jar up to inspect it. Then she lifted a log. The bottom of it was rotting and crumbling as she peered underneath. "Come to Mama!" she sang out. "Ow! *Ow!*"

****

With bags under both arms and more in both hands, John assumed his position on the beach. He scanned the sky.

"Sure hope this isn't the week they visit their cousins at the shore," he said to no one in particular.

****

Elaine licked her finger and raised it into the air, as she tried to figure out which way the wind was blowing. For the hundredth time that day she wished she'd paid closer attention when she'd taken sailing lessons at summer camp as a child.

****

Aunt Gladys went over and over everything in her mind. She also sat very still. From behind the door, she could hear Brogden's delighted voice.

"Good girl, Maggie!" he cried "You've got it!"

****

Brogden reached into a bucket and threw a handful of pellets into the tank.

"Yummmmmmmm!" Maggie rumbled. "Yummmmmmmmm!"

"That's right, you've earned your snack," Brogden told her. "Let's just hope you can remember what I've taught you."

Maggie flashed him a smile, showing all of her teeth, and rumbled with pleasure even louder.

"Yummmmmmmmmmm!"

****

Fred motioned to Nancy to slow down.

"Something's up!" he whispered.

****

"We've got her!" Simp hollered. "Look!" He wagged a finger at the monitor. The needle was going crazy. "Head west! Quickly!"

****

"They're picking up the pace," Nancy noted, beating her wings faster.

"Don't lose them!" Fred hollered back.

****

After practicing, Elaine brought the sailboat up onto the beach and sat down on the sand.

"I guess all I can do now is wait," she muttered nervously to herself.

****

John sat about twenty feet away from her on the beach, surrounded by the bags.

"That's right," he called to her, his voice shaking slightly. "Now we wait."

****

Aunt Hazel screwed the lid on the jar for the final

time and climbed the tree directly in front of the house. She settled down on the porch of a charming tree house and kept her eyes peeled on the ground below.

"Nothing to do but wait," she sighed.

****

"You all set in there?" Aunt Gladys called to Brogden.

"We're going to give it one more try, just to be on the safe side," he replied. "You?"

"Just waiting," she sang out, not budging.

****

The needle was almost pinned down to the top of the gauge.

"There! There!" Simp yelled. "That way! Turn!" His voice was high and squeaky with both disbelief and triumph.

"But there's an island right there!" Macky pointed out.

"Exactly! That's where she must be! On it, or under it, or around the other side of it. That's where they're hiding her!" Simp could barely get the words out fast enough.

Macky didn't need to be told twice. He lowered the throttle, and the bow of the boat rose into the air. Like a shark heading for its prey, it accelerated full speed toward the island.

****

"It's showtime!" Fred announced to Nancy. The two ducks flew ahead of the boat, quacking an alarm to

John and Elaine.

****

As the boat reached the waters surrounding Sunset Island. Macky manned the wheel while Simp opened a long black sack and removed several harpoons. Then he took out the rifle and tossed it to Macky.

"Be careful, it's loaded," Simp warned. His eyes had narrowed into sinister slits, like those of a tiger on the prowl.

Hanging onto the steering wheel with one hand, Macky caught the rifle in the other. The boat jumped up and over the choppy waves and thumped hard each time it landed in the water.

"Hey! Hold up!" Simp ordered. "Something's up there! In the water! Slow down!" Simp pointed in front of them. "What the—"

"Ducks!" Macky yelled. "It's ducks!" He tried to slow down but it was too late. Fred and Nancy were floating in the water, seemingly without a care in the world, directly in the path of the oncoming boat.

"I can't stop! We're gonna hit them!" Macky shouted. "Hang on! Move you lousy ducks! Move!"

"Don't hit them, you fool!" Simp yelled. "They'll get caught in the propeller or something!" He aimed at the ducks and threw one of the harpoons.

At the last possible second, Fred and Nancy beat their wings and rose into the air, but not before the spear of the harpoon crashed into Fred's right wing!

Simp let out a wicked cackle as he reeled in the

harpoon's line. It was covered with bright red blood and purple and brown feathers.

"Fred!" Nancy quacked. "Oh, my poor darling!" She landed and paddled over to where Fred lay floating, motionless, as the wake tossed him about.

"Oh, poor, poor Fred!" she sobbed.

****

"Slow er' down now!" Simp demanded as they approached the island through the narrow passageway on the north side. He held up a map of the lake that he'd found in the glove compartment of the boat. "There's low spots here."

"What's that up there?" Macky called out, gesturing to something ahead of them in the passageway.

"It's a danged sailboat!" Simp grunted.

The sailboat in front of them seemed to be in trouble. The sail was up, then down. It spun around in one direction, then the other. Several times it pitched at a dangerous angle, inches away from capsizing. It was entirely unclear where it was trying to go. Behind Simp's glasses, his beady eyes darted back and forth as he tried to discern the best way to get past it.

"Go left!" Simp ordered.

But when Macky steered that way, the sailboat abruptly moved to the left.

"No, no! Right!" Simp screeched. "Head right!"

Macky adjusted their course—and then the sailboat came about to the right. No matter which way they went, the sailboat followed, remaining in their path.

"Darn!" growled Simp. "That thing's nuts!"

On the sailboat, Elaine tried to remember everything she knew about the direction and speed of the wind and vectors and all the other factors of sailing, but her mind was overwhelmed with the jib and the boom and the rigging. She was unable to get the sailboat out of the way of the approaching speedboat.

"We're going to crash!" hollered Macky.

"Hey, watch it!" Elaine called over to them.

"*You* watch it, lady!" Simp retorted, his eyes wild.

Macky tried to turn the wheel, and at the last second he threw the boat into reverse...but it was too late. The sailboat tossed and turned and seemed to throw itself right at their boat. With an earsplitting crunch, the bow of the speedboat ripped into the side of the sailboat, and the force sent the boom into Elaine. It knocked her off her feet and straight into the water!

"Hey! Hey! Who do you think you are?!" she gasped and sputtered, shaking her fist at the men.

Macky and Simp ignored her and continued forward.

"We're almost there!" whooped Simp with one eye on the monitor and one eye on the island's beach. The crash had torn a large hole in the underside of the bow of the boat, and water was beginning to seep into the bottom. Macky pointed to the pool of water, which was rising rapidly.

"We'd better dock soon or we're going to go down!" he said to Simp.

Simp ignored him. His eyes were mad and glittering, fixed on the island.

"There!" he ordered. "That beach!"

Macky turned the boat toward the cove, and it shuddered violently as it unexpectedly hit bottom.

"What in the world?!" Macky screamed.

On the beach, John was feeding potato chips to a flock of seagulls who were relentlessly demanding more.

"Watch out for the rocks!" he called to the two men in the speedboat.

"We're sinking!" Macky called to him. "We're sinking!"

"Hold on!" John replied as he waded through the shallow water to the sinking speedboat. Then he said to them, "Do me a favor, would you? Jump out and feed my pet seagulls for me, and I'll pull your boat in. Deal?"

Macky and Simp nodded, then cut the engine and abandoned the boat. They scrambled over its side, standing knee-deep in the water. John tossed them each a bag of potato chips and began toward their boat. Immediately the seagulls swooped down upon the two men.

"More!" they screeched. "More!"

"You've got to *feed* them!" John instructed as he grabbed hold of one of the cleats on the side of the speedboat and began tugging it toward the beach. He caught sight of the harpoons and the rifle, and a shudder ran through him.

"Are you gentlemen out fishing or something?" he inquired politely.

"None of your business," sneered Simp.

"More! More!" the gulls continued to beg.

"Throw the chips faster!" John said. "They're hungry!" He continued towing the boat in.

"Hey...uh...." Macky said, shoving a handful of chips in his own mouth. "Ya' got any more of these?" Crumbs blew off his lips and into the air.

"Nope, that's it," replied John. He let go of the boat. It was too heavy to pull any further.

The gulls kept squawking for more. They swooped in closer to Macky and Simp in a frenzied swirl of thumping wings and pointy beaks.

"Hey! I'm almost out!" said Simp, peeking into the bag. "All I've got left are crumbs!"

"Me too," echoed Macky, his chin all greasy.

The greedy cries of the seagulls became frantic, and they began pecking at the empty bags.

"Call em' off!" Macky said, nervously. "Call em' off, man!"

John dove into the water and swam away just as the birds descended upon the two men, ripping the empty bags apart. Macky and Simp swatted and flailed at them trying to escape, but the seagulls were merciless.

"Help! Help!" Macky pleaded.

A shot rang out through the air.

Simp had managed to stumble to the boat. He had reached the rifle and frantically fired it. The startled birds scattered, flying off in all directions. The two men looked at each other, bewildered. They were scratched and covered in sticky, smelly bird droppings.

"Ew!" Macky whined and pointed to Simp. Simp wiped his glasses on his shirt and ran his fingers through his matted hair.

"Oh, never mind!" Simp sneered. "We've got no time to lose. I know that monster is in that house!" he proclaimed, pointing ahead. "Let's go!"

Dazed, Macky watched as Simp grabbed the harpoons and rifle and began pushing through the shallow water toward the beach.

"Come on!" Simp commanded. "This way!"

Macky trailed reluctantly along a few feet behind. They trudged up the beach, stumbled over the sand, and followed the tiled pathway. Then they stopped in front of the house.

"Now what?" Macky asked. "Are we going to break in?"

"No, we're going to ring the doorbell and ask them to politely lead us to the million- dollar loch baby." Simp shook his head in disgust. "Of course we're going to break in, you dimwit!"

"Ow!" Macky cried suddenly, slapping the back of his neck with his hand.

"How?!" Simp asked, exasperated. "Geez, do I have to explain everything to you? You're going to bang the door down!" Then he also gave out a forceful "Ow!" and began slapping at his arms. Soon they were both swatting at every part of their bodies.

A cloud of midgies had surrounded them.

"They're biting me like crazy!" Simp yelled.

"Me too!" Mackey screamed. "It's bloody biting midgies! *Ouch!!!*"

From the porch of the tree house high above them, Aunt Hazel shook the last of the midgies out of the jar and cheered silently as they rained down on the two men. It was a delight watching as they ran around crazily in circles, trying to escape the attack.

When the last of midgies had flown away, Macky and Simp dragged themselves onto the porch. Head to toe, every bit of their exposed skin was rapidly swelling into red, itchy bumps.

****

With one well-placed kick, Macky broke the front door in. A moment later the two men were standing in John and Elaine's living room.

"Let's split up," Simp said. "Look for any clues to where they're hiding the little loch baby. I'll bet you anything the little monster's swimming in a tank somewhere in this house."

He kept the harpoon, handed the rifle off to Macky, and ran up the staircase to the second floor. Macky strolled into the kitchen but didn't find any tanks. He did, however, discover a warm crock-pot filled with chili, and he stuck his finger in to sample it.

"Hmmmmm…not bad," he said, licking his lips. Next he conducted a thorough search of the living room and dining room. No tank there, either.

Then Simp hollered down from the floor above

him. "Hey! I think I've got something!"

Macky bounded up the stairs, then paused when he couldn't figure out where Simp had gone.

"In here!" Simp called. He was in the room with all the maps and stacks of containers. Simp had opened one of the containers and was holding a pellet in the palm of his hand. It broke apart easily, and he sniffed it.

"Loch baby food," he said. "I'm sure of it."

Just then a rumble shook the house, and Macky and Simp froze.

"What...what was that?" Macky whispered.

"It's our million-dollar monster, of course." Simp said sarcastically. "She must be calling for her mama," They heard the rumbling again, this time much louder, and the floor vibrated beneath them.

Simp raced down to the first floor, then rifled through every room in search of a door that would lead to the basement. It took him only a matter of seconds to find it in the kitchen. He tiptoed down the stairs, confident that he was on the right path because the rumbling grew more intense with each step he took. *Surely I must be close now*, he thought gleefully.

Macky followed at his heels. Being a heftier man, however, he found it hard to tiptoe. He worried that his clodding, clunking footsteps would surely alert anyone that they were on their way into the basement.

"Shhhhh!" Simp turned around and frowned at him.

When Simp reached the bottom of the staircase, he

came to an abrupt halt. It was dark in the basement, and Macky bumped right into Simp's back.

"Geez!" Simp whirled around, more than a little annoyed. "For cripe's sake, watch it, will ya?"

"Sorry!" Macky apologized. Then he said, "Hey, I don't see nothing down here. No tanks at all."

Rumble.

Rumble....

RUMBLE!

Macky's face turned white.

"There's nothing down here, see?" he said nervously. "I think we should just get outta here."

He turned to head back up the staircase, but Simp stopped him by grabbing onto his shirt collar.

"Hold on just a second," Simp said. He reached inside his pocket and produced a thin, pen-sized flashlight. "I've got this, so calm down."

He shined the light all around the room—across the floor, along the ceiling, and into the corners. Then the beam settled on the bureau.

"Help me move that," he ordered Macky. They moaned and groaned as they shoved it a few feet across the floor.

"Well looky here," Simp snickered. "Appears we found ourselves the gatekeeper. Or should I say...the tank guard?"

There, with her back to the secret door and caught in the blinding light with eyes wide as saucers, sat Aunt Gladys.

CHAPTER 15

Captured!

Simp ambled slowly over to the door and squatted down in front of the tiny woman. She stared up at the strange-looking man, who was covered in droppings and red welts. She could see herself reflected in his glasses.

"Hello, little lady…and I do mean little." He burst out into a wicked cackle.

Aunt Gladys said nothing.

He reached over her head and gripped the padlock in his hands. He twisted it and pulled at it and turned it and shook it from side to side in frustration.

"It's locked," he said to Macky.

Macky shrugged his shoulders.
"Whaddaya want me to do? Break another door down? How come it's always me whose gotta damage the property?"

Rumble.

Simp put his palm to the door.

Rumble.

"She's in there! I know it!" he said. Then he turned his attention back to Aunt Gladys.

"Okay Granny, where's the key?"

His voice was rougher now, and he slammed the point of the harpoon into the floor beside her. She jumped and shook with fright.

"I...I don't have it," she croaked.

Rumble....

RUMBLE!!!

"C'mon Simp," Macky said, "you heard the lady. She doesn't have it. Let's get out of here. This place is giving me the creeps." Truth be told, he didn't like the idea of being mean to the little old lady. She kind of reminded him of his own grandmother, just smaller.

Simp spun around angrily and moved until he stood eye to eye with Macky.

"If you want to leave, that's fine with me," he snorted, "but don't expect me to share a single cent with you."

Turning back to Aunt Gladys, he continued with, "So whaddaya say? Whaddaya say you open that door so I can get a looksee at what's behind it? Cause we all know what's behind it don't we, Granny? A little monster that's going to make me richer than I've ever been in my wildest dreams!"

"No," said Aunt Gladys firmly.

"What...did...you...say?" he asked, incredulous at the audacity of the wee woman.

"She said no. Just leave her alone," Macky repeated. "I'm telling you I don't have a good feeling about this. Let's just go."

"Shut *up*, Macky!" hollered Simp, backhanding him on the side of his head. Macky slumped to the floor, and the rifle he'd been holding clattered away. Simp picked it up and pointed it at Aunt Gladys. She was shivering like a leaf in the wind.

"I'm going to say this very nicely and only one more time," he announced through clenched teeth. A vein on his forehead was visibly pulsing. "Open...it...."

Rumble....

"Open it, Granny, or—"

"Aunt Gladys?" Brogden's voice came from the other side of the door. "Aunt Gladys, are you okay?

"Oh, sure, Brogden. Fine, really. Never been better. It's just...." she hesitated.

"What is it, Aunt Gladys?" he asked.

"It's just that there is a man out here who wants to get in. And...." she faltered. "And he has a gun!"

"A gun?" Brogden shrieked. "A gun?"

"Yes, a gun you parrot!" Simp sneered. "And if your auntie here doesn't open the door right this minute—"

"Aunt Gladys, open the door!" Brogden ordered.

"No, Brogden. I won't," she stated.

"Do it!" he pleaded.

"No. I promised John and Elaine that I wouldn't."

"Aunt Gladys, please, just open it. Everything will be okay. I promise you," he said.

"Look, this is all very touching, but time's a wasting," said Simp. "I'm going to count to three, and if you don't open the door by then...." He motioned to indicate the harpoon and the rifle. "At least I'll give you the choice of which I use on you."

Aunt Gladys's throat bobbed as she swallowed

hard, her eyes bright with terror.

"One," Simp said in an oily voice that made Aunt Gladys' skin crawl.

"No," she told him, crossing her arms.

"Two...." Simp said, eyes glazed behind his glasses.

"No." She repeated.

"Do it, Aunt Gladys!" Brogden sobbed. "I'm begging you! I can't lose you!"

"Three!" he said sharply—and still Aunt Gladys did not move.

Simp used neither the gun nor the harpoon. Instead, he reached down, picked up Aunt Gladys in his fist, and flung her aside. She flew through the air, hit the wall, and slumped to the floor, motionless.

"Aha!" Simp said then, grinning broadly.

Aunt Gladys had been sitting on top of a tiny key. He scooped it up and inserted it into the lock. It made a tiny popping sound as it snapped open. He yanked the lock off, the door swung open, and the cool, watery scent of the rolled over him.

"Okay, now we're getting somewhere!" he said joyously as he began descending the stairs.

Rumble.

Rumble....

"All my life," he muttered to himself. "I've waited for this moment. Dreamed of it."

There were just a few steps left.

"Come to Papa, you little monster! Come make Papa a rich, rich man!"

He got to the cement wall at the bottom and raced around it triumphantly, brandishing the harpoon high above his head.

Then he stopped.

The dark green, murky water of the tank was still and empty. Not a bubble. Not a ripple. Not a wave. The rumbling sound had ceased, and the silence was deafeningly eerie.

Simp walked up to the tank and stood there scratching his head.

"That's strange…I thought…." he mumbled. "Where is she?"

He wheeled around, and his beady eyes darted from side to side.

"I heard a voice in here, too, so I know someone is in here!" he hollered. "Where are you?"

He waited, but there was still no movement, still no sounds.

"Come out, come out, wherever you are!" he sang out in a high-pitched voice.

Nothing.

He pressed his forehead against the tank's cool glass. *I'm so close now*, he thought. *I'm sure of it.*

Simp strained his eyes trying to gain a glimpse of something—anything—inside the murkiness. He wiped his glasses on his shirt and rubbed the lenses until they were clean. Just as he was about to turn away, he noticed something out of the corner of his eye. A small, almost imperceptible stream of bubbles rising to the surface.

He gripped the harpoon tightly.

"I've got you now, you little monster!" His voice rose excitedly. "Show yourself! I have no fear of you! I demand it! Show yourself!"

Nothing.

More silence.

"Darn it!" he cried, banging on the front of the tank.

Just then, one of the containers that was stacked against the wall toppled over and rolled to a stop at his feet.

"What in the world? Who's there?"

His eyes searched all around as his heart pounded like a bass drum. But he saw no one. He stared at the container for a moment, then a smile spread slowly across his face.

"That's it!" he said, nodding. "A little snack might do the trick. Yep! It's feeding time at the zoo!"

He bent down to the container and started to lift its lid, when it suddenly popped off and flew into the air!

"Now, Maggie, now!" Brogden commanded, leaping from the container where he had been hiding. "NOW!" he repeated at the top of his lungs.

Simp found himself unable to move. His overloaded mind couldn't decide what was more shocking, the foot-high boy with the long neck, or the fearsome beast with the long neck—and who was rapidly slithering over the top of the tank as its snake-like head reached toward him!

"ROARRRRRRRRRRRRRRRR!!!"

Simp looked in horror into Maggie's wide-open mouth. Row upon row of glinting, spiky teeth were moving quickly in his direction!

"Aaaaaahhhh!" Simp shrieked.

"*AAAAAHHHHHH!!!*"

"*ROARRRRRRRRRRRRRRR!!!*"

Maggie's tail thrashed from side to side, drenching both Brogden and Simp. She snapped her mouth open and shut as she moved closer and closer to Simp. He stumbled backwards, tripped over the pail, scrambled back onto his feet, and stood shaking with his back against the wall. Then he remembered his harpoon.

"Back off!" he yelled at Maggie, holding it with the point out. "Back off, I tell you! All those years ago, your mother, Morag, almost killed one of my uncles. And no one believed him! People said he was crazy! A fool!" Simp paused to catch his breath. "Well, the time has come for revenge! I will reveal you to the world and everyone will know the truth! People will see you for the monster you are! And I will be rich!" He heaved the harpoon through the air toward the tank.

It wasn't until a moment later that Simp realized his mistake. In his rage, he had forgotten to hold onto the rope that was tied to the harpoon. He watched with a mixture of terror and disbelief as the rope uncoiled and danced like a wild snake in the air. He tried to grab the end of it, but it was too late. The harpoon hit the water first and the attached rope floated down into the tank after it.

"Uh oh," he muttered as Maggie, who had avoided

being hit by the harpoon with a quick twisting move, glared at him and prepared to strike. Now without a weapon, Simp watched as her great neck once again rose above the top of the tank, her jaws wide and moving swiftly toward him!

"ROARRRRRRRRRRRRRRRR!!!"

"Good girl, Maggie!" cried Brogden from where he had hidden behind all the other containers.

Simp ducked to the right as the giant creature's mouth snapped shut. He could feel her hot breath and then a flashing pain as several of his hairs were plucked out. Letting out a yowl, he realized that he had no choice but to attempt an escape, because the next time the monster lunged at him it would be more than just a few hairs—it would be his head!

But before he went, he had an idea....

He eyed Maggie warily, trying to figure out how best to make a run for it. Then he caught sight of a black plastic bag in the corner of the room. He snatched it up and grinned.

"Okay, so maybe I can't get *you* this time, you beast. But there's still another way to get the money. I'm sure a zoo or a lab will pay for *your little friend*!"

He lunged in the direction of the containers, brusquely knocking them aside and away from Brogden. Several of them popped open, and the pellets rolled out across the floor. Brogden tried to run, but Simp was too fast. He grabbed him Brogden the waist and dropped him into the bag. Brogden screamed and twisted frantically in a futile attempt to free himself.

"ROARRRRRRRRRRRRRRRR!!!"

Maggie continued snapping her jaws, but Simp dodged and swerved, evading her ferocious teeth.

"Let me out! Let me out!" sobbed Brogden from inside the bag.

"Let me out!" Simp mimicked after he managed to scoot around the cement wall and out of Maggie's reach. He slung the bag over his shoulder "Oh, I'll let you out," Simp snickered. "I promise. And when I do, I will be a much richer man!"

He pushed the small door open, strode past the still-unconscious Aunt Gladys and Macky, raced up the stairs two at a time, and rushed to the front door.

Then he stopped again.

"Uh oh...." he said flatly.

The sailboat woman and the seagull man were standing there with a policeman. In a flash, the seagull man yanked the black bag away from him, and the policeman pulled his hands behind his back.

"You're under arrest," the policeman said just before the handcuffs clicked into place.

CHAPTER 16

THREE MONTHS LATER

"Teamwork," Elaine said proudly. "That's what saved Maggie!"

They were all there—John, Elaine, Aunt Hazel, Aunt Gladys and Fred—having a nighttime party on the beach. Nancy would have been there, too, but she was busy sitting on the nest. John had lit a dozen torches, and they cast a festive light around the group.

"Do you think they'll ever come back?" Fred asked. His voice was filled with concern. Shortly after the police had taken Simp and Macky away in the police boat, a distraught Nancy had arrived on the beach, where she had related Fred's dire medical condition. John had immediately taken a kayak out to rescue him. When John found him, Fred was weak from blood loss, but no bones were broken and, after recuperating among the reeds on the beach for a few weeks, he was good as new.

"No, I don't think Simp and Macky will return to Sunset Island," Elaine reassured him. "They'll be in jail for quite a long time."

As bad as she felt about the damage to her sailboat from the crash, Varick (remember him, from the marina?) felt even worse when he saw the state of *his* boat, which was almost completely underwater by the time the police located it. Evidently, Simp and Macky had stolen it. So when the police captured them, their list of crimes grew even longer—boat theft, damage to property, and speeding on Lake Wahkmo.

"Well, that's good," Fred replied, "because I have a happy announcement. At last count, four of the six eggs have hatched, and the other two are pipping as we speak. Three girls and a boy so far," he stated proudly.

"How wonderful!" Aunt Hazel crooned. "I just love babies! Why, I remember when Brogden was a tiny baby...." She launched into a story about Brogden's first words and first steps and first tooth as the festivities stretched long into the late night hours.

The weeks following Maggie's rescue had been a relaxing vacation for all of them. Aunt Hazel had spent the days exploring the island, collecting flora and fauna samples. She steered clear of the midgies though, having gotten one too many bites herself during her part of the plan.

Aunt Gladys had luckily gotten off with only a severe headache after being thrown against the wall. She stayed close to Elaine during her time on the island. They spent many hours in the kitchen, sharing recipes and other cooking ideas. Even though everyone had proclaimed her a hero, she told Elaine (when they were in the middle of making soufflés) that she didn't feel like a one.

"I should have fought Simp," she confessed wistfully. "Then he wouldn't have gotten the key."

"Darling, he had a gun!" Elaine said. "And a

harpoon! Goodness knows, none of us could have predicted that. And, given his size, you were awfully brave." Gladys blushed at this flattery.

Brogden had enjoyed the visit most of all. No one could believe that he had trained Maggie to act so ferociously in such a short time. Although he knew that Maggie would never have actually attacked Simp, Brogden really enjoyed watching Simp *think* it would happen. *Served him right*, Brogden thought.

When Simp and Macky had been led away, Brogden climbed out of the black bag and rushed downstairs to check on Maggie. She was in a terrible state after seeing him get bagged and carried off. To console herself, she had reached as far out of the tank as she could and ate all the pellets that had rolled out onto the floor. When she saw that Brogden was safe and sound, she tried to turn somersaults but only managed one because her tummy was so full. Then she smiled her big, toothy grin at Brogden.

"Good girl, Maggie," Brogden praised her. "Good job."

"Yummmmmmmm!" she replied. "Yummmmmmmmmm—*burp*!" Then she rolled onto her back and fell asleep.

Brogden spent the rest of his time on the island taking care of Maggie and teaching her tricks. Each day he reflected on how thankful he was that she was safe; that they all were.

Macky was still groggy when the police led him away. Dazed, he'd rambled on incoherently about some little lady who was only about a foot tall.

"Only a foot tall and she's in trouble!" he repeated over and over to the officers, trying to convince them. "I'm telling you, there's a foot-high old lady in this house!"

"Right, sure," the policeman said. "And I'm the Easter Bunny. Keep walking. You can tell them all about it down at the station." Aunt Gladys even managed to feel a little sorry for Macky.

"I do believe he was trying to do the right thing," she decided in the end. "He just got mixed up with the wrong person."

That person was Simp—and the policeman hadn't believed him, either.

"Let's get this straight...." the officer said. "You're telling me there's a monster with rows of pointy teeth in a tank under the basement of this house?"

"Yeah, that's right," Simp responded.

The policeman shook his head. "I hear plenty of wild stories," he said with a laugh while talking with John and Elaine later on. "It's the nature of the job, I suppose. But this is a new one." They nodded and laughed, too, inwardly relieved that the officer hadn't decided to investigate the basement...or the black bag, for that matter.

"Yes, it's true," Elaine said from her chair on the beach that warm evening. "Maggie wouldn't have been rescued without each one of us." Then she smiled suddenly, "Oh, look! Here they come!"

She pointed to Brogden, who was sitting on top of Maggie's middle hump as she swam through the dark waves. They were about thirty feet from the shore, circling the island. Brogden waved a greeting as they passed by, then they disappeared around the bend.

Brogden had asked John and Elaine if he could ride Maggie during the daytime, but they said not yet, because there were too many people who would still misunderstand her and want to capture her or harm her.

Riding Maggie around the island felt like the greatest thing in the world to Brogden. (Certainly better than a boat, he thought.) He held tightly onto her shining scales as she dipped up and down. From time to time, she would blow streams of water high into the air through her nostrils. Each time she completed a lap around the island, she would turn to face Brogden, and he would toss a pellet into her mouth.

"*Yummmmmmmmm....*" she hummed gratefully. "*Yummmmmmmmm....*"

Brogden knew he would miss her. But there was no question in his mind that he had to return to his home by the swale. His aunts needed him. They loved him. And he loved them. But John and Elaine promised him that he could return whenever he wanted. He could consider Sunset Island his second home, they said.

A thick, gray cloud slipped in front of the moon, and for a minute the night was pitch black except for the stars. Years later, people who were looking out at Lake Wahkmo that night would recall rubbing their eyes and wondering what it was out there, moving through the water near the island. Some said it was a group of large turtles.

Others argued it was a string of boats. From a distance, with only the naked eye, it could have been anything. Anything at all.

But on that night, if they had thought to reach for their binoculars, they would have seen Maggie—a most unusual and magnificent creature, swimming gracefully through the waves, her scales glittering like an explosion of light. And on her back was a young boy named Brogden, all of a foot tall, who always believed it he ever went down the swale, he would find something incredible.

Afterword

A quick online search will bring up many tales of sightings and encounters with Morag, the "monster" of Loch Morar, Scotland. I first learned of her while reading *The Search for Morag* (1974) by Elizabeth Montgomery Campbell and David Solomon.

The characters of Macky and Simp are based on two friends named Duncan McDonnell and William Simpson. They claimed that on the evening of August 16, 1969 they were returning from a fishing trip in Loch Morar when a creature 20-30 feet in length slammed into their boat. McDonnell tried to attack it with an oar, and Simpson fired a shot at it with his rifle, which caused it to disappear under the water. Later they reported that the creature had rough, dirty brown skin, three humps, and a snakelike head.

About the Author

Valerie Munro is a School Library Media Specialist and has had a lifelong love affair with books. She studied writing at Columbia University Teacher's College and received a Geraldine Dodge Foundation writing scholarship to the Fine Arts Work Center in Provincetown, MA. Her short story *Hallowed Ground* won First Prize at the UCCC MacKay Library, and she has also written articles for journals and magazines. She lives in Sparta, NJ with her husband, two children, and many pets.

This is her first book.

Made in the USA
Lexington, KY
09 August 2017